Witch & Wizard
THE FIRE

Witch & Wizard
THE FIRE

James Patterson
and Jill Dembowski

Published by Young Arrow, 2011

2 4 6 8 10 9 7 5 3 1

Copyright © James Patterson, 2011

Excerpts of poetry in this work are from the following public-domain
sources: page 5, excerpted from 'The Mask of Anarchy' by Percy Bysshe Shelley;
page 38, excerpted from 'Death at the Window' by Robert Fuller Murray; page 50,
excerpted from 'A Hand-Mirror' by Walt Whitman

First published in Great Britain in 2011 by
Young Arrow
Random House, 20 Vauxhall Bridge Road,
London SW1V 2SA

www.randomhouse.co.uk

Addresses for companies within The Random House Group Limited can be found at:
www.randomhouse.co.uk/offices.htm

The Random House Group Limited Reg. No. 954009

A CIP catalogue record for this book
is available from the British Library

Hardback ISBN 9780099544173
Trade paperback ISBN 9780099544180

The Random House Group Limited supports The Forest Stewardship Council
(FSC®), the leading international forest certification organisation. Our books
carrying the FSC label are printed on FSC® certified paper. FSC is the only forest
certification scheme endorsed by the leading environmental organisations,
including Greenpeace. Our paper procurement policy can be found at:
www.randomhouse.co.uk/environment

Printed in Great Britain by Clays Ltd, St Ives plc

For Jack, who started me down this
long, twisted, magical road.
You will be king one day,
and you'll be a very good king.
—J.P.

For Bobbie Dembowski, who taught me the magic of
words, and Mark Dembowski, who cheers louder than
any foolball fan. ILYIHYNDYTBPITWW!
—J.D.

Welcome to your worst nightmare,
or maybe one you can't even imagine.
A world where everything has changed.
There are no books, no movies,
no music, no free speech.
Everyone under eighteen is distrusted.
You and your family could be taken
away and imprisoned at any time.
Your very being is expendable,
even unwanted.

What world is this? Where could
something like this have happened?
That's hardly the point.

The point is that it DID happen.
It's happening to us right now.
And if you don't stop and pay attention,
it could happen in your world next.

Whit

YOU WANT A FAIRY TALE, don't you? Well, I'm not sure I can give you that.

You can find adventure here, that much is true. There's magic, too, and murder and intrigue. And there is a man more wicked, more ruthless, than any monster or madman lurking in your grimmest childhood nightmares.

But there are no heroes. I can't be that for you—not anymore, not after everything that's happened.

It went like this.

There was a great orator, smart and charismatic. Crowds came from every corner of the Overworld, hypnotized by his promises. They called him The One Who Is The One for a reason: he was the one who would change the world. It wasn't until he took everything away that the people even knew what they'd had.

First we watched our books burn, the gray tendrils of smoke choking out our protests. Then our art and our music disappeared, and the rest of our freedoms weren't far behind. Red banners stretched up over the tallest buildings, and ash rained down with bombs. Prisons overflowed with children, and when they were released, they were no longer just kids but dead-eyed warriors trained in torture.

It was for the greater good, The One said. The "New Order," he called it.

The Prophecies talk about two people who will alter the course of this history. A girl and a boy, a witch and a wizard. My sister and I, Wisty and Whit Allgood. It was as surprising to us as much as to anyone. Terrifying, even.

We tried to be your heroes, tried to live up to that destiny. With our newfound powers, we offered hope. We joined the Resistance movement and infiltrated the prisons. We protested the New Order and advocated for peace.

But after the last bombing, my sister and all of our freedom fighters were scattered like seeds in the wind, the entire Resistance crumbling. Even our parents went up in smoke. Their cries still echo in my ears.

So I had no one left. I thought I had nothing left to give. But then came the plague. It was my last chance to make a difference. I walked into homes that smelled of death and seethed with disease. I carried bleeding children into clinics and shelters. And in one of those clinics, I found my sister working as a nurse, helping as I had, hoping as I did for a better future.

But then Wisty got sick, too.

Now, The One Who Is The One's eyes, playful and cruel, look down mockingly at me from the billboards. I'd thought we could fight him. I'd thought we could win. I guess I was wrong. You see, without both Wisty and me, there is no history, no future, no hope.

And she's dying.

So here we are. This is the end. This is no fairy tale, and there is no "happily ever after." Our world does not end when you close the book. Our world is real. Too real. It sounds like children shrieking in the darkness and soldiers' boots thundering through the streets. It smells of sewage and disease and defeat. It feels like the weight of my sister writhing in my arms.

It tastes of blood.

BOOK ONE

BLOOD HOLIDAY

Chapter 1

Whit

MY LUNGS ARE bursting, and if she dies, I'll die.

We're tearing through the cramped, dank streets of the capital, running for our lives from the New Order police and their trained wolves. My calves are burning, my shoulders ache, and my mind is numb from all that's happened.

There is no more freedom. So there is no escape.

I stumble through this strange, awful world we have inherited, past a mass of the sick who are shuddering from more than just the cold. A man collapses at my feet, and I have to wrestle my arm away from a woman holding a baby and pointing at me, shrieking, "The One has judged! He has judged you!"

And then there's the blood. Mothers scratch at open pustules, and children cough into rags stained red. Half the poor in this city are dying from the Blood Plague.

And my sister is one of them.

Wisty's even paler than usual, and her slight frame is

curled over my back, her thin arms wrapped around my neck. She's in agony; her breath comes in gasps. She's murmuring about Mom and Dad, and it's ripping my heart right out of my chest.

The street pulses with waves of vacant-eyed citizens scurrying to work. A guy in a suit shoulders me to the curb, and an old man who seems to recognize me slurs something about "dark arts" under his breath and hurls a glob of spit at my cheek. Everyone has been brainwashed or brutalized into conformity. I can hear the shrieks from the abused populace as the goons hammer through them just a block behind.

They're gaining on us.

I can picture the wolves straining against their chains, foam building on their jagged teeth as they yank our pursuers forward. All missing fur and rotting flesh, they're Satan's guard dogs come to life. Something tells me that if—or when—the New Order police catch us, those animals aren't exactly going to go easy.

There's got to be an open door or a shop to slip into, but all I can see are the imposing, blaringly red banners of propaganda plastering every building. We are literally surrounded by the New Order.

Now they're right on us. The cop in the lead is a little zealot who looks like a ferret. His face is beet red under an official hat with the N.O. insignia on it. He's screaming my name and wielding a metal baton that looks like it would feel really awesome smashing across my shins.

Or through my skull.

No. I will not go out like this. *We* have the power. I think of Mom and Dad, of their faces as the smoke streaked toward them. We will avenge them. I feel a rush of rebel inspiration as lines of a banned poem thunder in my head along with the soldiers' boots.

"Rise like Lions after slumber / In unvanquishable number." I put my head down, hike up Wisty, and surge forward through the plague-ridden crowds. I won't give up.

"Shake your chains to earth like dew." I break away from the crowd, seeing an opening at the end of the street. *"Which in sleep had fallen on you— / Ye are many—they are few."* We used to be many, when the Resistance was thriving. Their faces flash before me: Janine, Emmet, Sasha, Jamilla. And Margo. Poor Margo. Our friends are long gone.

Now it's just me.

I burst through the mouth of the alley into a huge square. A mob of people gathers, looking around expectantly. Then a dozen fifty-foot-tall high-definition screens light up, surrounding us and broadcasting the latest New Order news feed. With everyone distracted, it's the perfect time to find a way out of this death trap. But I can't tear my eyes away from this particular broadcast.

It's a replay of footage from my parents' public execution.

My head swims as Mom and Dad look down from all around us, trying to be brave as they face the hateful crowd. And as I watch the people I love most in the world go up in smoke for the second time, I hear Wisty's hysterical, delirious ramblings.

"No!" She flails in my arms, trying to reach out for them just like she did that day. "Help them, Whit!" she shrieks. "We've got to help them!"

She thinks she is watching our parents' *actual execution* again.

Before I can soothe my sister, she's hacking, and I feel something hot and wet oozing down my neck and shoulders. I gag back my own bile, but the most horrific part of all is that the mess dripping down my sides is full of blood.

She hasn't got much time left.

Chapter 2

Whit

I'VE GOT TO get Wisty somewhere safe—like, *now*. We seem to have lost the club-wielding pigs behind the crowd for a few precious seconds, so I whirl around to find another alleyway...and nearly run smack into my own face. I stumble backward, chills running down my spine.

And then I see them.

A hundred posters, or a thousand, on every pole and window. Wisty and me.

WISTERIA ROSE ALLGOOD and
WHITFORD P. ALLGOOD.
WITCH AND WIZARD.
HIGHLY DANGEROUS CRIMINALS.
WANTED ALIVE.
MOSTLY DEAD ACCEPTABLE.

I whip around again, hyperventilating. I feel eyes on me everywhere. An old woman grins up at me with a mouthful of missing teeth. A couple of suits trot down the white marble steps of the Capitol building, their cigars pointed our way. There's a little girl standing off to the side, her wide, gray eyes boring into me. She *knows*.

They all know.

Right on cue, the squad storms through the entrance to the square, their heads flicking around in search of us. And then, like something out of a horror movie, the zombie wolves start to howl.

There's a small, partially bombed-out stone building down a side street that I can spot from here, and it looks promising. Or at least more promising than the jaws of the half-dead mutts. I slink toward it as inconspicuously as possible and slip in through a side door.

A gargantuan painting of The One Who Is The One greets me, his bald head and Technicolor eyes bearing down, and a sign on the wall reads: CONFESS YOUR CRIMES TO THE NEW ORDER AND YOU WILL BE SPARED. THE ONE ALREADY KNOWS ALL. There are bullet shells on the floor.

This could be . . . really bad.

But there's no one here. We're safe — for now.

My shoulders and lower back muscles are screaming, so I finally slide my sister down to the floor. She looks like the image of death. I sit her up in my lap. "Come on, Wisty," I plead, wiping her face with my shirt. "Stay with me."

Her red hair is matted with sweat, but her teeth are

chattering. I hold her clammy hand, whisper the words of some of my surefire healing spells over her, and add every ounce of hope I have into the mix.

Only . . . nothing works.

How can my power be bone-dry? I'm a wizard, but I can't even save my sister. She's my constant, my best friend. I can't just sit here and watch her get weaker, watch her eyes puff up as the blood leaks into them, watch her float in and out of consciousness until her world finally goes dark. I can't keep watching the people I care about most die.

I already did that.

Twice.

I wince, thinking of Mom and Dad. *If they'd only taught me a bit more about how to wield this power before . . .*

I can't finish the thought.

It's not just a problem with my power, I'm sure of it. There's something in the air here in the capital—like The One poisoned it or something—and it's turning the New Order followers into empty, nodding pod people, and the poor, potential dissenters into writhing, moaning Blood Plague victims.

The survival rates haven't been high.

"Why did you have to volunteer at that stupid plague camp and get sick, Wisty?" I whisper-shout at her through angry tears. "We've seen what The One can do, and if he wants every single freethinker in the ghetto to get sick, then no amount of healing spells is going to make you immune!"

I *need* my sister, the often annoying know-it-all, rebel leader, greatest threat to the New Order, unexpectedly rockin' musician, witch extraordinaire....I can't do this alone. No—I can't do this without *her*. She was the only one I had left in the world.

My breath catches in my throat. I've already been thinking of Wisty in the past tense.

I feel everything within me explode at once. I smash my hand into the painting of The One, but it's as if it's made of metal, and my hand throbs in agony.

"I wouldn't do that if I were you," a voice says from the door. I whip around to find a young soldier seemingly dressed in his daddy's too-big uniform, pointing a gun at me from the entrance.

I almost laugh. *This* is the twerp who's bringing us in?

"Yeah, I kind of figured that out now, thanks," I say, cradling my injured hand. I look behind him. No one seems to have followed him here.

"On behalf of the New Order and in the name of The One Who Is The One"—he looks up at the painting reverently—"I demand that you surrender your power and turn over The One Who Has The Gift."

He means Wisty. The One wants her fire. I take a couple of steps toward my sister protectively. The barrel of the gun follows, trained between my eyes.

"Freeze, wizard," his adolescent voice cracks. "One more step and I blow you from here to the next dimension." It's like he's been rehearsing his lines on action figures.

"I've been to the next dimension, actually," I quip. "The Shadowland's not so bad." Even with my hurt hand, I could easily deck him, if I could just get a few steps closer.

At my nonchalance, his expression changes to one of sour insolence. He evidently decides to up the ante. "Or I could just kill *her* instead," he says, swinging the gun toward Wisty. "They might even give me a medal."

They wouldn't. They'd be furious that he destroyed the potential of so much power, and probably execute him on the spot. I don't say this, though; the eager way he's fingering the trigger has my attention.

"Hey, now. No need to overreact," I say, putting my hands up. "Let's all just remain calm." I try to keep my voice even.

Boy soldier, brainwashed. When the first kill still feels like a game, when it still seems as if the victim will sit up afterward and ask to play again.

But Wisty won't.

Silence hangs thick between us as the kid debates between his conscience and his pride. I already know which will win, which always wins. His eyes narrow on the mark, his finger tightening. I start to sweat, ready to leap in front of my sister.

But before I get that far, his eyes flutter—and he crumples to the ground.

I let out a long breath. *What just happened? Did my power suddenly flare up and go rogue? Did I have a perfectly targeted spasm of some kind?*

No. Something had nailed him in the back of the head. I spot an object rolling to a stop nearby. A *snow globe?*

In the entryway behind him is that same big-eyed, grim-faced little girl who was watching me in the square. She looks fierce, her tiny mouth twisting in annoyance.

The expression kind of reminds me of Wisty at the height of her frustration with me. The girl is standing outside the door, beckoning me into the alleyway.

"You just gonna gawk at me, wizard boy? I've got more where that came from, if you need a little nap."

Chapter 3

Whit

"YOU HAVE TWO choices," the pint-size vigilante professes.

I look at her warily. There's no telling if she's really on my side. They've used kids to get to us before, and there are almost no rebels left in the capital. There's a reward for our capture, no doubt; maybe she's got dark motives.

She's filthy and bone-thin, but she's got this strangely confident expression. And—weirder—she's wearing antlers.

Then it sinks in: the Holiday.

In my panic I must've missed the details. Though celebrating the Holiday is forbidden under pain of death, I now see hints of it everywhere as I glance out the window: ribbons clipped to New Order flags, candles winking from windowsills, and the kind of ice sculptures that Wisty and Mom went nuts for—only these are shimmering tributes to The One.

"You have two choices," the little girl repeats impatiently. "And they are *your* choices, and yours alone."

She's got her hands on her hips, her round, silvery eyes glaring out of her tiny face. She's probably around seven or eight, but her eyes look way older, like those of the wizened elves Wisty and I used to read about in the Necklace King series—back when we got a kick out of fantasy books and didn't know we *actually had* magical powers.

"You can either come with me or let the red-haired girl die. It's no big thing for me," the little fountain of goodwill says, like death is something she's intimately familiar with, even bored by. "You should dump her and save yourself." She eyes Wisty and frowns. "That's what I'd do."

Chapter 4

Whit

"PEARL MARIE NEEDERMAN," she huffs, making no effort to shake hands. "My place isn't far."

Against my better judgment, I follow the kid out behind the building and duck into an alley roped off with a sign that reads: QUARANTINE ZONE. Still, dragging my dying sister back through the N.O. squaddie-packed capital square doesn't exactly seem like a better option.

Pearl Marie is small but lightning quick, even though she's lugging a large bag. With Wisty in my arms, I have trouble keeping up as the little girl slips under fences and around street carts, Holiday antlers bobbing.

There are no people in the street except for Blood Plague sufferers, and more than one suspicious face slams a door and draws the blinds as we pass. Maybe I'd take it as an insult if I weren't still dripping with Wisty's vomit.

After less than half a mile the police are on our trail again, smashing their clubs through abandoned food stands and hurling insults at our backs. But the plague victims are constantly underfoot—and crave vengeance. I turn to see a herd of the sick descend on a couple of soldiers, the men's howls muffled as they're pulled down into a pit.

Pigeons scare up as fear-stricken shrieks echo down the alley, and soon we no longer hear the crush of boots on pavement. Many of the policemen are turning back.

Or are now infected.

The maze of turns is dizzying, and Wisty's getting heavier and heavier. But even with the cops off our tail for the moment, Pearl jets along, seemingly running in circles, like a greyhound that just can't stop chasing a rabbit.

Just as I'm about to protest and ditch this kid, she wheels around and says, "Here." What she's pointing at looks like a demolished pile of rubble.

"Um, I hate to break it to you, Pearl Marie, but it kind of looks like the New Order bomb strikes got to your home first."

The kid sighs like I've totally disappointed her. "You're not really a wizard, are you? It's over here, stupid."

I follow her and maneuver Wisty through the narrow side entrance into a one-room, dismal basement apartment. I have to duck to get through the doorway. There's almost no light, and it smells of mothballs and disinfectant.

Pearl Marie lowers her sack and motions to our surroundings. "You can just drop the witch anywhere, really," she says, like my sister is a coat or a pair of shoes.

"Where is...everyone else?" I note the scraps of blankets and bedding covering the floor. It's clear that a lot of people have been living here for a while.

Pearl laughs ruefully. "Oh, they're all out doing things that are actually important. You know—scavenging for necessities, things to save our family, not whispering hocus-pocus or waving their fingers around like lightning is gonna zap out of 'em."

I narrow my eyes. I realize I'm not in top form at the moment, but who *is* this girl? "Look, we can leave right now—"

"No, stay." Her face softens. "Everyone will be home soon. And I have something to show you—what I've been collecting all day. They gave me the biggest job of anyone." She beams.

I'm expecting food or blankets or beans she might've lifted from the purse of some New Order drone to buy medi-salves or to bribe soldiers with. But Pearl opens the sack so reverently that for a second I think it must be something really important—even more than money, like a baby or a puppy or something. It's...

Holiday decorations? Make that *broken* Holiday decorations.

Of course. Now the snow globe makes sense. And the antlers.

"Aren't they...beautiful?" Pearl whispers in awe. I nod. I have to admit they kind of are beautiful, all shimmering shattered glass and colorful broken lights.

Still, I'm getting antsy. The decorations are nice and all,

but this kid is a piece of work. My sister is *dying* here. Wisty's tossing on the floor, ripping at the blankets in anguish, and Pearl keeps staring intently at the broken lights as if they hold secret powers. Finally she notices my agitation and sets the sack aside carefully. Then she fishes out some moldy-looking rags and wets them from one of the buckets set up to catch ceiling leaks.

Pearl puts a compress on my sister's forehead. It's all I can do to keep it together when Wisty moans, "Mama. Just let me die. Please. Just let me die."

"Oh, you will," whispers Pearl Marie. "You will."

Chapter 5

Whit

I'M ABOUT TO tell off Pearl Marie for her cruel pronouncement when the door slams open. Instinctively I tense up in an offensive position.

But this posse isn't N.O. It's family. I can hardly blink before Pearl disappears in a sea of embracing bodies, and a big hand grasps my shoulder and spins me around.

An older gray-haired man looks me up and down and shakes his head. "Mama May isn't going to like this one bit," he warns, his face serious, but I can see that his eyes are more amused than angry. Before I can ask who Mama May is, he spots Wisty in the corner, blood all over the front of her shirt, and winces.

"That your girl? In bad shape, isn't she?"

"My sister." I nod, not sure if I can say anything else without totally losing it in front of this man.

"She's a trouper." There's a long, silent moment between

us that seems to acknowledge just how screwed Wisty really is.

Too long. Too silent. I notice a group of women across the room with the same dark, lank hair as Pearl. They're all giving me sidelong looks and whispering.

They hate us, I think. *They're all just waiting for Wisty to die so they can go back to feeling at least a little bit safer.*

I'm almost starting to resent this man, but then he grabs my hand in the strongest handshake I've ever felt and looks at me intensely. "I'm Hewitt," he says. "If you need anything, don't hesitate to ask." He glances at the women staring at us and chuckles. "Don't mind them. They're just paranoid. Mama May will set it right."

Mama May, I soon learn, is Pearl Marie's mom. The moment she enters the room, it gets warmer. She takes up space. Literally. Her big girth is a sharp contrast to the rest of her spaghetti-legged family, but she's also got presence. Her full, hearty laugh could almost make me believe we're not orphaned in a world controlled by a psychopath with a God complex. It could almost make me believe we're *home.*

But Mama May takes one look at Wisty and me, and her face blanches, and she frowns so deeply she looks like a big, disapproving grouper.

"Pearl, honey, c'mere. I'm not so sure this is the best idea..." Mama May cocks an eyebrow in Wisty's direction. "We've lost so many to the Blood Plague already, and with them being wanted and all..."

Pearl puts on a face of such innocent longing it almost looks like a mask; it's a face only a youngest child can master. "Mama, please let them stay. If we were going to get the plague, we'd all have it by now. And look at her. She'll probably die in a few minutes anyway."

I notice she brushes right over the fact that we're wanted fugitives.

Pearl's hands are on her hips, and her big eyes are pleading. Even against Mama May, she's certainly got clout, and even before she says, "It's the Holiday. We have to do the right thing," I know Mama will cave.

Half an hour later, despite Mama May's ruling in our favor, most of Pearl's dozen or so family members are still glaring at me with nervous hostility. I mean, they look like every other family that has gone through hardship under the N.O.: they have deep creases in their faces from watching their children carted off to disciplinary prisons; bruises under their eyes from sleepless nights, expecting raids; and with no more music, art, or expression in the world, their muscles don't remember how to smile. But there's something else, too. They look straight-up terrified.

It's the eyes. That silvery gray is mesmerizing and demands accountability, and I can't look away. They're haunted. I pull Pearl off to the side and gesture at the onlookers.

"Hey, what's going on?" I ask. "What's everyone afraid of? I mean, I realize we're wanted criminals, but they know nobody knows we're here, right?"

She glares back at me fiercely. "What do you mean,

what's everyone afraid of? What is everybody in the entire Overworld afraid of? It's not about you being on the run. It's because you've been involved with *him*."

"You mean The One? But why would he—" I want to say that surely the Needermans are small potatoes to the New Order. They're not Resistance anyway.

"Shh!" she hisses, eyes wild. "We don't say *that* name in this house." She grips my arm and drags me over to a corner, even farther away from the others, but there's an audible increase in whispering.

"We're almost all that's left," Pearl says gravely. I look at her, not understanding, and she gestures impatiently around the room at the candles, the figures, the signs of their devout religion. "The only ones who still believe in the Holiday and everything it stands for, who still keep the faith," she says. "And his spies are everywhere."

"But there must be other people who still…practice," I press, thinking of the illegal Holiday decorations present in the square, the obvious signs that there are other religious families still holding on.

She shakes her head. "Everyone just believes in *him* now. In the beginning, we gathered in one of the halls. We thought we'd be safe there, that they'd respect the holiness of the place. Instead it just made us a giant target. He sent his henchman to do his dirty work."

Pearl looks mesmerized, as if she's watching the events unfold in a movie. "One of them had learned some of his evil magic. He wanted to put his hands on our heads. Some of the kids went right up to him, because it was like being blessed, like we were used to at the hall. I stayed behind, but not my brother, not Zig. Ziggy was smart, but he had more faith than any of us." Pearl smiles faintly, remembering, but then her expression darkens.

"And the evil man—he wouldn't stop smiling—put his hand on Ziggy's forehead. Ziggy was smiling, too. And... and then Ziggy's face... it started..." She swallows, her eyes unfocused. "*Melting...* just *melting off*." She takes a breath. "I kept screaming for Ziggy, but... then someone grabbed me. And then we were running. That's all I remember."

I'm almost too horrified to speak. Pearl is staring straight ahead, her mouth a thin line.

"But you're here now," I say. "You're safe."

She laughs, and it's cold, harsh. "Yeah. Safe..."

I look around at the frightened faces, the spooked eyes, and I finally get it. I'm one of the dark ones, with this terrific power I possess. My magic makes me *like him,* regardless of how I use it.

Hewitt approaches us and looks at Pearl's angry little face. He raises an eyebrow at me but lets it go. "Here." He hands me a sorry-looking candle made of some kind of fat. "We light these every night. For the dead. We're about to begin."

I want to ask Pearl more questions—about Ziggy, and above all about the horrifying smiling man who melts children's faces. But she's already standing up to join her family in a big circle. And it's clear from that determined expression setting her lips in a tight little knot that that's the last she's ever going to say about poor Ziggy Neederman.

Chapter 6

Wisty

IT'S LIKE I'M swimming, my long red hair swirling around me. I'm swimming, only my goggles are foggy and my air tank has just run out of oxygen. My lungs are burning so much I think for a second that I might be flaming out and can actually *feel* it for the first time. The girl who can set herself on fire. Some Gift.

There seems to be a ton of people surrounding me, and none of them looks like my brother. Where is Whit? I vaguely remember him carrying me, but what's happened since then? Is he sick? Is he being tortured somewhere by my skeletal captors?

Two kids stand over me, prodding my arm with a stick. The bigger one, a freckle-faced show-off with a chipped tooth, is answering a question the other has asked.

"She's the red-haired witch, dummy. Not very good at it, is she?"

I focus through the pain and summon all my energy to

fix the little braggart with a long, withering look. To my utter satisfaction, the kids scamper away in horror. "She'll change us into rodents!" Freckles yells. Ah, my reputation has preceded me. Somehow, it feels like an overwhelming relief that I can still strike fear into the hearts of children.

Exhausted, I collapse back into the cushion of sleep.

The next time I open my eyes, it's dark, and there are candles everywhere. Everyone in the room looks shell-shocked, like they've just received the worst news. My heart starts to race until I see my brother. He's across the room, standing with some grubby-looking little girl, and I feel such a sense of relief I almost pass out again. I wish I could get his attention, but I don't have the strength to move.

An older man with a weathered face and a braid running down his back is leading some kind of vigil. These people, whoever they are, have lost someone. My heart aches for them; I know what loss feels like, too.

Believe me.

"Let's not let them take everything from us yet, though." The weathered man looks from face to face, eyes fierce. "Let's sing for family. Let's sing for hope."

The crowd of filthy, gaunt survivors all hold hands, and there's barely enough space in this tiny basement room to fit them all. The whole place is radiant with candlelight, and the broken glass dangling from the ceiling shimmers.

Then the singing starts up.

It's low at first, and then, as more and more voices join in, the volume builds, like the vibrations of a bell or the mournful echo when you trace a finger along the lip of a glass. You feel it inside you.

It's so beautiful, you almost have to turn away.

When I realize what they are singing, it's like an arrow to my chest. "Silent, Silent." Even buried under all this grief, I can see Dad's expressive face mouthing the words over our heads on Holiday Eve, hear Mom's sweet voice dancing along the verses. A sob catches in my throat as I hum along to the familiar melody, tears streaming down my cheeks.

I lock eyes with Whit across the room. He's looking at me like his heart is breaking, like he's saying good-bye. To me. I shake my head. *No. No.*

The candles are blurring again, I'm drowning in darkness.

Silent, silent.

But I'm not ready to go.

Not yet.

Chapter 7

Whit

I AWAKE DISORIENTED in cold, damp darkness, my body aching, my sister nowhere in sight. There are shadowy figures all around me, but I can't make them out. Something jabs me in the ribs and I flip onto my feet, muscles tensed, ready to tear it to shreds. In the millisecond before I move to strike, there's a hyena-like laugh, high and mocking.

"Ooooh," a familiar young voice teases, "someone is a *leetle* bit jumpy this morning. Come on, wiz boy, let's get going." I make out Pearl Marie's mop of ratty hair in the darkness, and yesterday comes flooding back to me. I must've passed out on a pile of rags.

"Go? Go where? It's still dark out!" I groan. What with being a fugitive on the run from the most powerful being in the universe, rewatching our parents' execution, and carrying my dying sister on my back through a maze of plague victims and trained wolves, I've been put through the wringer, physically and emotionally. I could sleep until *next* Holiday season.

"It's half past quit-your-whining o'clock." Pearl Marie is already crouched down, digging through the rags. "You're fit to work, ain't ya?" The tiny drill sergeant starts lobbing bedding at my head.

"Well, yeah, but—"

A moth-eaten sweater soars through the air. "Gotta"— warped sun hat to the gut—"pull your weight, like everybody else. Find a disguise." I duck as a shredded blanket makes a beeline for my nose. Pearl stands up, hands on her hips. "Everyone knows your stupid face."

"What about Wisty?" I protest. "I can't just leave her—"

"No prob." Pearl shrugs. "Mama May told me to stick close to the house and look after her." I soften a bit at the mention of Mama May, remembering how much the Needermans are risking by taking us in, how dearly they'll pay should they be found out. I owe them this.

I reluctantly start climbing into the crusty clothing. After a minute, I peek out from under my disguise of toga-like moldy blanket topped with a half-unraveled scarf as a face mask topped with a large sun hat. "Does it still look like me?"

"Big muscles? Small brain? Yep, I can definitely still tell it's you under there." Pearl frowns.

I sigh in frustration. It used to be so easy before. I could just morph a bit, take the form of an old man, a bird, almost anything I'd need to be. . . .

Wait a minute. Something is different. Pearl's looking at

me in wonder, and I feel things shifting: the shape of my nose, the length of my hair...and are those dimples I feel? Pearl holds up a piece of Holiday glass so I can see my reflection.

I'm stunned. After days of feeling my power slipping away from me, I can't believe it freaking worked! *Who's got the mojo? Wizard's got the mojo!*

Meanwhile, Pearl's doubled over with laughter.

"Brandon Michael Hatfield?" she snorts. "Are you *serious?*"

"What?" I reply, incredulous. "You know him?"

"Brandon. Michael. Hatfield!" Pearl's voice goes up a full octave. "Of course I know him!" she shrieks. "He was the biggest dreamboat in the former Freeland! I just didn't realize you had the mind of a preteen girl!"

Celebrities have mostly been wiped out in the N.O. regime for representing idols other than The One, so what's the harm in making use of likenesses of long-gone pop stars? Besides, I've been the poster boy for public scorn long enough. Maybe I wouldn't mind having a face everyone *likes* for a change. So sue me.

"My girlfriend used to be into his music," I say, shrugging, pretending that the mention of Celia doesn't still hurt somewhere deep inside. Pearl nods skeptically. "Hey, it's actually pretty tough to just come up with a new identity out of thin air! Sometimes you have to, you know, *borrow* one. Brendan What's-His-Face seemed like as good an option as anyone else."

"Brandon Michael Hatfield," she corrects, as if I've committed sacrilege.

"Got it." I roll my eyes. "Anyway, it works, doesn't it?"

Pearl nods, still giggling, then hustles me toward the door. "You better get goin'."

"But my sister..." I glimpse Wisty's frail body across the room, her red hair matted with fever. If anything, she looks worse today.

"I'll tend to her for you. I'll talk to her and dab at her forehead. Trust me. I'll look after her." Pearl pats my hand and peers up at me with her big silver eyes, all scout's honor. I start to smile gratefully, but then Pearl finishes, "At least until she dies."

Chapter 8

Whit

I'M TEARING THROUGH the streets, madly searching for an escape from this sad and tragic world. And it does seem mad that I'm trying to get to a place where the dead still walk. To the Underworld. To the Shadowland. *To Celia,* the love of my life, trapped among the Lost Ones.

I can't get Pearl's words—"until she dies"—out of my head. If I could just get back to Celia, I know she could tell me what to do. She'd been brutally murdered by the New Order, but she sometimes still came to visit me. As a spirit. And she had helped Wisty and me so many times before.

She'd know what to say. Wouldn't she?

I don't care. I need her now, no matter what. Her sweet smell, her comforting arms, her voice whispering encouragement. I can't be alone now.

Like I'd done so many times before, I head for a concrete wall at the end of an alleyway and smash my shoulder into it at full force, hoping for some vulnerability I can't see, a bend in the fabric of this dimension giving way to the next. We'd used this pathway before, in the days when it seemed portals to the Shadowland were everywhere. But The One's influence is growing, and many portals have disappeared or have been blocked.

Like this one.

I'm met with only a bright flash of pain, and I crumple to the ground, utterly defeated, yearning for Celia, for my parents, for the kids who gave their lives for the Resistance. I've lost nearly everything, and now I'm going to lose my sister, too.

The words lap at my ears like an echo in a seashell. "Until she dies..."

No. Not yet. I drag myself out of the garbage on the street.

I will not let my sister die.

Chapter 9

Whit

I PULL MYSELF up, new energy coursing through me.

I'm thinking of the Resistance fighters, of Janine and Margo and Emmet—kids who had lost everything but who would never give up on one another, and never gave up on us. Kids who are long gone now but whose determination I can still feel.

I'm also thinking of Byron, whom Wisty zapped into a weasel on more than one occasion. As screwed up as a lot of his theories were, Byron seemed to be right about one thing: when our power went through him, it became stronger, even though he didn't possess any magic on his own. We'd tested that on other kids, too, and it had seemed to work. So maybe, just maybe, it could work now?

I sprint back to the Needermans' bombed-out apartment building, taking the basement stairs two at a time, and then burst into the small room, searching for Pearl.

She's nowhere to be found. What was it she said? *I'll look after her. Trust me.*

I'm not sure I know the meaning of that word anymore.

I crouch down by Wisty. She's still feverish and barely conscious, and her face is filthy.

"Don't give up on me yet, Wist. I've got a plan. Just hang in there." I start to wipe my sister's face with a dirty cloth when the door opens and the little ragamuffin saunters in.

Pearl sees my angry expression and shrugs. "I got hungry and figured the witch wouldn't miss me," she says cheerfully enough. "Shouldn't be long now anyway—the mess she coughed up earlier was some kind of gross black sludge."

Before I know what I'm doing, I bat the scraps of food Pearl's holding to the floor and tug the little girl across the room toward my sister.

"Hey!" she protests. "It's not my fault she's—"

"You're not going to watch over Wisty until she dies. You're going to help me make her better," I tell her, voice as hard as iron. "Right now."

35

Chapter 10

Whit

ON THE CEMENT floor in the drab basement apartment, Wisty struggles in the grubby linens, her breath coming in quick, jagged gasps. Sweat stands out on my sister's forehead, but her teeth chatter behind her papery lips.

This *has* to work.

Pearl slouches next to me, feigning boredom, but I'm gripping one of her hands and one of Wisty's with frenzied determination. Wisty coughs violently, and red drops of blood appear on the corners of her mouth.

I lick my lips and try to swallow my panic. I have to work fast; we're losing her.

I let go of Pearl and start to riffle through my journal for a spell, but Pearl snatches the book away with nimble fingers practiced in theft.

"*Poems?*" The kid looks genuinely appalled.

"Give it. Now," I manage. It's taking a massive effort not to yell at her.

"Fine," she says, chucking the journal at my head. "I'll just be over here, choking on my own vomit."

"That's what my dying sister is *actually* doing right now, thanks to your lack of cooperation." I heave a frustrated sigh.

I lean over to pull Wisty's fire-red hair away from her clammy cheeks. "Listen, Wist, you're not done living— not by a long shot," I say quietly. "You're not done rocking the music, bursting into flames like a badass, or mouthing off when I'm trying to give you advice. And this is the best advice your big brother is ever going to give you." I start to choke up but force this last part out anyway, because I need my sister to hear it: "You're not allowed to die yet, okay? It's definitely not in your best interest."

Wisty doesn't move and her breathing stays shallow, but Pearl's face softens and she gets this big-eyed sympathetic look, like she might actually start crying, too.

"I have something to say." Pearl awkwardly puts a hand on Wisty's shoulder, looking kind of embarrassed. I'm staring, not sure what to make of this, and she shoots me an annoyed look. "Close your eyes, Whit. It's like a prayer or whatever." I shut my eyes obediently and hear her settle in beside me.

I expect her to make some snide remark, but when she speaks, her voice is sad and sincere. "Whit seems to care about you a whole lot," Pearl starts. "I had a brother, too, who I cared about. And he used to keep an eye out for me, too." She's quiet for a moment. "But he's gone now and—" Her voice quivers, and my heart lurches in my chest. "And it was just the worst thing that's ever happened to me, so I know how he feels."

Pearl pauses for a moment, as if deciding whether or not to go on. "So just…just wake up already. Amen." I open my eyes, but Wisty's pale face is unmoving.

Pearl grips my hand tightly as if it had been her idea all along. "Okay, wizard," she says gently, "*now* do your sappy poetry thing."

I flip to a fresh page in my journal, and Murry Robinson's words unfold on the page before me:

> *Though Death but seldom turns aside*
> *From those he means to take,*
> *He would not yet our hearts divide,*
> *For love and pity's sake.*

I shut my eyes tightly, and a shudder goes through me as I imagine the blurred, skeletal image of Death pointing a spindly finger at Wisty, then turning away in defeat.

He looks more like The One, actually.

The anger builds within me until I'm shaking with all of the rage, pain, and frustration that comes from losing everything you love in the world. I say the poem over and over, my voice forceful and sure, and I hear Pearl chanting beside me, too, her words warped by tears for Ziggy and the others whom Death didn't turn away from.

Energy surges through us into Wisty's frail body, and

the single lightbulb in the room flickers and shatters. My fingers burn with the spark of raw, healing power.

When the surge subsides, I peek at Wisty tentatively. I hold my breath, waiting to see the effects of my power, the color rushing into her cheeks, the familiar wry smile, her own magic emanating from her again. It has to have worked. I *felt* it.

But she's not moving. I'm not even sure she's breathing.

My pulse quickens. It's like...she's already gone. Pearl is looking at me with big, nervous eyes. What if whatever I just did actually killed Wisty instead of saved her?

And then, just as I'm ready to give up all hope, my sister's eyelids flutter open.

I don't know what I was expecting—lucidity, maybe? The magic hasn't made Wisty shiny and new again, or even totally well, but still, something has changed. Her eyes are dazed and feverish, burning into mine.

And they're no longer ringed with red.

"Wisty!" I shout, squeezing her way too roughly in a hug I can't stop.

"Hi, Whit," she chokes out. "I'm...okay." Tears slip down her cheeks, and I'm nearly sobbing with relief myself. With that small effort, Wisty passes out, but sheer, unfiltered joy floods through my system anyway. Somehow I know she's going to make it.

I have the power to heal. This is what it's like to feel invincible.

Chapter 11

Wisty

IT'S COLD. SO, so cold.

I'm wrapped in blankets, but I'm as icy as a slab of beef hanging in a meat truck: chilled to the bone. The air tastes stale and recycled, but I can't even seem to lift my head to get a better look at this room.

My vision is still a little blurry, but I'm suddenly aware of a figure next to me. I flinch, adrenaline rushing to my head as my body sends out the alert: Stranger. Dark, claustrophobic room. So many people want me dead. And where is my brother?

I squint to focus my eyes.

It's just a kid, I realize with relief. Her eyes are glued to me, a little smile on her grimy face. She has this weird beauty to her, and for a second I think she might be an angel.

Then I see the glint of her knife.

I try to lurch away from her, but my body won't obey. I

feel paralyzed. I try to scream for help, but it comes out as a raspy, gurgling moan. The kid raises an amused eyebrow at me. *I'm drugged,* I think. *She's drugged me and is about to carve me up.*

She moves toward me. Not knowing what else to do, I grip the covers with white-knuckle panic. A whimper escapes my lips.

"Relaaax," the girl says, her round, gray eyes inches from my face. They're almost hypnotic; I'm still afraid, but I find myself automatically calming down. She sits cross-legged next to me and starts whittling at splinters of wood, the edge of the knife catching the low light of the single candle. I try to slow the blood thundering into my brain, and after a minute she looks up.

"So, you're finally awake. People were placing bets that you'd be dead before sunrise, you know," she says matter-of-factly.

I stare at this morbid little girl, not sure at all what to make of her.

"When Whit brought you in, he said he didn't know how much longer you'd last. But thanks to *my* help, you pulled through."

"How—?" I cough, then start again. "How do you know my brother?" My vocal cords are hoarse from disuse, and my voice comes out as more of a squeak than the threat I had intended.

The big-eyed girl definitely doesn't appear threatened. She prattles on for what seems like forever, relating the list of everything she knows about me and my brother—like how our faces are plastered on every wall in the capital—but I can't seem to focus on her words.

My heart constricts when she gets to the part about how our parents really are dead, but I'm too numb with cold to process much else, and her animated descriptions of deadly Holiday ornaments, the poetry cure, and blood in the streets have my head spinning.

I feel totally drained, like all the blood, energy, power... all the *magic,* has been sucked right out of me. *My hands are blue* is the only thing I keep thinking. If I could just get warm, work up a little magic, I could figure all of this out.

"Come here for a sec," I croak, interrupting the girl's tirade.

I must sound utterly crazy, because the kid looks like there's absolutely no way she's getting any closer to me right now.

"Come on. Want me to cough some blood your way? Just get over here and help me sit up," I prod.

She reluctantly moves closer and tries to push up the rags behind me with the very tips of her fingers so she can avoid actually touching me. Whatever. If I'm going to die, maybe I can at least warm up a bit first.

I point a finger at the fireplace and catch my companion's skeptical look. I feel a twinge of anger, that familiar heat. That does it. A terrific fire crackles in the hearth, the three-foot flames instantly warming up this damp room.

"Yes!" I give a little uncontrollable squeak of victory. I may not be totally well, but my magic is coming back.

The girl is evidently impressed. "Whoa!" she says with a twinge of awe that makes me way more proud than I should be for just a little fire. "You really are a witch."

"And a scary witch, little girl," I bite back with a self-satisfied smirk, though I'm already collapsing into the rags, exhausted. "Lucky for you, you didn't try to use that knife."

The kid smiles. "It's for cutting kindling. I wasn't going to slice and dice you." Her fingers dance tauntingly over the handle of the weapon. "It's the Holiday, after all."

Chapter 12

Whit

I SET OUT this morning looking like Brandon Michael Hatfield again, still elated with the miracle of Wisty's recovery and confident I could coax the rich, wasteful citizens of the New Order capital to throw me at least enough change to show the Needermans my appreciation. But after three hours on a busy corner in the business district with only a meager handful of beans to show for it, I'm losing faith.

It dawns on me that I haven't really seen much traffic in a while. This morning, herds of businessmen filed by (never mind that their vacant eyes looked right through me), but now, around lunchtime, when my little corner should be jumpin', there's hardly anyone.

Glancing around, I notice that, save for the bored-looking lunch-cart man, I am actually the only person on this block. A newspaper blows across the street like tumbleweed. There might as well be crickets, the road is so quiet.

I stand up, uneasy. This is the middle of the most frenzied, commercial place in the entire capital. Was I so swept up in self-pity I didn't notice things getting seriously weird around here?

Then I hear a laugh down the block, and out of the corner of my eye I notice two smartly dressed, cheery men slipping onto a side street. Curiosity piqued, I amble after them, leaving my cardboard sign in the dust.

Rounding the corner of the alley, I'm totally unprepared for what I find.

The smell hits me first.

That *smell*. The nauseating stench of burning flesh and singed hair hangs in the air with the plume of black smoke.

I cough, eyes watering. It's almost unbearable.

At first I don't understand where it's coming from. All I see is a large group of New Order citizens, mostly businesspeople, impeccably dressed in sharp suits and mile-high heels, shouting gleefully, apparently enjoying some sort of rally during their lunch break.

Then I see it—*her*—the thing they're all standing around. In the center, tied to a post, is what looks like a large piece of meat, still smoking. The blackened, pulpy form at the stake doesn't register at first. My mind can't make the connection between a living, breathing human being and *that*.

And then I see a tuft of hair clinging to the charred scalp, and my head starts spinning.

Not a rally—a witch burning.

My throat goes dry, and I feel paralyzed with horror. I'd heard the rumors, but I'd never imagined there could be people like this. I mean, the men and women who make up the group before me—the mob—just look so normal. Followers of the N.O., yes. Richer than most, certainly. But still they look like people you see every single day in the capital, people with families and jobs. People with some speck of compassion, surely.

Until you see the emptiness in their eyes.

Who knows who this doomed woman was, or if she even possessed any magic at all? The New Order, with its bold red banners blanketing the Overworld, feeds on bloodlust.

These are its children.

Reality finally comes into sharp focus, and my heart races. I stumble forward, frothing with fury and purpose. "Stop!" I shriek, which feels incredibly insufficient. But what else is there to say?

I'm too late, of course.

Then an icy, deep-down fear wraps tightly around my heart and wrings out my breath. The screams I hear now don't belong to the woman; they're the sickening war cries of a mob gone mad. Because they're turning. The frenzied group is turning from the crisp remains of the poor soul strapped to the pillar.

And they're turning on *me*.

Chapter 13

Whit

TIME STOPS, AND every muscle in my body tenses as hundreds zero in on me like bloodthirsty piranhas, ready to pick me clean to the bone.

"Aren't you...Brandon Michael Hatfield?" a woman asks, awe creeping into her voice.

I let out a long breath, nodding. I'd forgotten about the spell.

My relief lasts only a second, though, since the next thing I hear is a whistle. Out of the corner of my eye I see a van pull up, but just as I register what the words painted on the side—N.O. SANITATION SQUAD—actually mean (*sanitation,* as in *wiped out*...as in one of The One's infamous Death Squads), a billy club smashes into my right temple.

My vision returns just in time to see a steel-toed boot connect with my abdomen, knocking the wind out of me and making me feel like I could puke up a kidney.

Or all of my large and small intestines.

The crowd pulses and sways in front of me as a man with a greasy black mustache and thin little lips, seemingly the leader, yanks my hair back, his cold eyes inches from my face.

"By order of The One," he spits, reading from an official-looking paper, "all scum shall hereby be cleaned from these Orderly streets, including practitioners of the forbidden dark or expressive arts, those individuals formerly known as *celebrities,* and all others posing a threat to the integrity of the New Order." He scowls, taking in my mask of Brandon Michael Hatfield's chiseled features—apparently almost as offensive as my real identity. "And that includes *you,* scum."

I manage to cough up enough phlegm to douse him with a good spray in return, which I'll probably regret in about five seconds.

The other Death Squaddies move in, and now the real party begins.

One yanks my arms behind my back while two more take turns kneading my face into pizza dough, blood pouring from my nose like marinara. Things are happening too fast for me to register the pain of each injury, but as I'm wrenched to the side I *definitely* feel my bad shoulder dislocate from its socket, the bright pain shooting through me like an ax.

I could attempt to hurl a spell at them to hold them off, but something tells me that life will be much, much worse if they know who I really am. I try to focus on something else besides the fists raining down on me, but the only other thing I can see is the murderous mob just beyond the soldiers' circle.

A woman in a mink stole and garish lipstick shouts at them to "finish him off!" and the image of the witch's smoking corpse flashes in my memory.

I'm not ready to be "finished off" quite yet. Even with Celia waiting for me in the Shadowland.

Celia. The thought of her is like another kick to the gut, but imagining her sweet smile and her warmth—and remembering exactly *who* took her from me—is enough for some vengeful spells to come to mind.

There's no choice now but to rely on the magic, which is pretty, well, *stressful,* considering point-and-click hasn't exactly been working for me lately.

Celes, I might be seeing you sooner than I thought.

Chapter 14

Whit

I'M NOT MUCH more than a bloody pulp on the ground at this point, but I hurl every ounce of magic I've got left in me at these brutes. I'm mumbling through chants and curses and poems, forcing out everything negative I can muster.

And it's kind of... terrifying.

I feel this dark energy building within me, growing into a power that needs to get out and find a target. I finish with a poem that always seemed particularly gruesome:

> No more a flashing eye — no more a sonorous voice
>   or springy step;
> Now some slave's eye, voice, hands, step,
> A drunkard's breath, unwholesome eater's face,
>   venerealee's flesh,
> Lungs rotting away piecemeal, stomach sour and
>   cankerous,
> Joints rheumatic, bowels clogged with abomination...

Before I can finish Wallace Shipton's words, the New Order thugs double over, spewing their lunches across their shiny black boots, and blood dribbles out of the citizens' lips, staining their fine clothes.

"The Blood Plague!" I slur through swollen lips. "They're all contaminated!"

When this registers, the citizens and squaddies, equally panicked, quickly and brutally turn on one another. I limp away from the chaos just as the beatings start, soldiers and businesspeople scrabbling like dogs, all trying to go for the jugular.

I pause for a second on the corner, listening to the cries coming from the alley. Guilt at having created even more violence eats at me; this isn't the sort of work the Prophecies intended, I'm sure of it. I hesitate and consider going back to heal them all.

Then I think of that pitiful, blackened form strapped to the stake, and my heart hardens with a bitter new understanding of the world we're living in. Let them destroy one another.

I allow my disguise to fall away as I walk. But somehow I still don't feel like myself.

Chapter 15

Wisty

THERE'S NO POWER, and outside the soldiers of the New Order occupation continue to brutalize the citizenry. But inside the Needermans' candlelit basement hovel, the spirit of the Holiday season warms us right down to our souls — and it's been a very long time since Whit and I felt anything resembling spiritual warmth.

Mama May flashes her biggest smile at all of us and bangs on a bucket to signal that the meal is ready. An excited murmur goes through the room.

"Come on, come on! Everybody gather round," Mama May booms excitedly. "We've got a very special Feast Day celebration tonight. Something we haven't had in almost a month: meat."

A cheer erupts from the group, and the starving Neederman family members settle into a circle on the floor, looking up expectantly.

Mama May reveals two poorly plucked pigeons, skinny

as sparrows. They look like another family has already picked them over. I stare at Whit pointedly.

"It looks delicious, Mama," Pearl says with authority, and everyone murmurs in polite agreement.

Mama May kisses the top of Pearl's head and starts hacking into the birds, and I know I should be grateful and I know I should honor their tradition, but I see the sadness in all of these big, silver eyes and the hunger in these thin, strained faces, and I just...

Can't. Take it.

I start to say something, but Whit puts a hand on my arm and shakes his head. He's been weird and moody since he came back from begging. He was limping and bleeding but wouldn't say why. In fact, he's barely said a word to anyone all night. I'm about to tell him that he's seriously cramping the Holiday vibe, but then...he does something wonderful.

With a flick of my brother's wrist, we've got thick rolls drenched in butter and mashed potatoes full of sour cream. An oversize turkey dominates the middle of the circle, and creamed corn edges up on green beans.

And the pie. Apple, pumpkin, pecan. I could eat pie for the rest of my life.

The kids are all talking at once, and the adults are looking too dumbstruck to really believe it. I beam at Whit excitedly, but he's not smiling. Instead he's watching Pearl, who's still slicing at the tough pigeon meat on her plate, her mouth twisted into that tight little knot I keep spotting on her face.

No one moves to touch anything before Mama May's say-so, and I can tell Whit's as nervous as I am.

But Mama's round face glows, candlelight dancing in her eyes, and her broad grin puts me at ease. "I can't tell you how much this means to our family. We've lost so much—" She looks around at each hollow-cheeked kid and takes a deep breath. "I just want you all to know that this really is the best Feast Day we've ever had."

I think of past Holidays with food I never really tasted, presents I can't even remember. Cutting out of family time early to do one thing or another. I squeeze my brother's hand.

"It's the best for us, too," I whisper.

Chapter 16

Wisty

AFTER DINNER, WHIT keeps pushing for us to just take off, leaving the Needermans behind.

I gawk at him. "*Now?* You're not serious. It's the Feast Day!"

He chews his lip. "Wist, you haven't been outside in a while—you don't know how it is. Things are getting more dangerous." There's something different in his voice that I can't place. He looks away from me, but he's already gathering our things.

"Well, then there'll be more N.O. guards around now than ever, won't there?" I point out. "Besides, I'm barely over the plague." I try to look frail. Using my near-death experience is a little manipulative, but it's true nonetheless.

Can't we just enjoy this semblance of happy tradition a tiny bit longer? my eyes plead.

Whit huffs and stalks away, but I know I've at least bought us some time.

Still, later, as the Needermans exchange their Holiday gifts, I almost wish we had left and avoided intruding on their intimate family moment. Whit and I try to give them space, cleaning up the dishes on the sidelines, but it's hard not to stare at their thoughtful handmade presents— metal trinkets they unearthed while scavenging; rocks polished smooth; drumsticks whittled from scrap wood by hand....My heart clenches at the unexpected reminder of the gift my mom once gave me.

Just then Pearl Marie runs up to us, a ball of excitement. She's holding out a garbage bag tied with string for each of us. I take mine, raising an eyebrow at Whit.

"What are you waiting for? The fall of the New Order? Open it already!" Pearl squeals.

At the bottom of each giant garbage bag is a single strand of silver tinsel. I'm not quite sure what to do with it, but Pearl's eyes shimmer expectantly, and Whit's face lights up. I haven't seen him smile this wide since...well, since before we were first kidnapped.

"Thanks, kid. This really means a lot." From the way Whit's acting, it's clear how precious this scraggly stuff is to her and how tough it must've been to give it up.

"Yeah, well, I figured you might need a little sparkle for that ugly mug," Pearl says, straight-faced.

"Come here, smart stuff!" Whit yells, scooping her up and tossing her in the air. Pearl shrieks her high hyena laugh, and it's almost like we're a family.

Family. Suddenly I miss my parents so much I can

almost feel them in the room with me. We were together not so long ago, but it already seems like forever since I've heard their voices.

Voices that The One silenced for good.

Before I can turn away, Mama May spots the hot, salty tears rushing down my cheeks. Her strong arms envelop me in a crushing hug.

"I know how it is, sweet pea. Everything's changing, and this time of year is the hardest. So many traditions lost, so many people dead. It used to be the season for getting together, loving your neighbor. Would you believe we couldn't even find a meeting place to read the Holiday legends? It's a disgrace, is what it is."

She's absentmindedly combing her fingers through my hair as she talks, like I've seen her do with her children. I normally hate to have my hair touched, but it's surprisingly soothing to feel her strong hands kneading my scalp. I feel safe.

"What about the hall? That's where my family always heard the readings," I say, tracing my hand along the neat braid she's somehow made of my tangled strands.

"It's gotten a lot worse lately," Hewitt explains, walking up with Whit. He hands each of us a dessert plate heaped with pie. "They're cracking down on anyone caught believing in any greater power other than *his*. After all those people were executed in the square last month, the hall is pretty much defunct."

Mama May shakes her head and sets aside her pie slice

untouched. "Besides, you can't find anybody who'll say a strong word against *him* anymore, let alone folks who want to pray for better days." Her eyes are brimming.

Pearl tugs at her mother's dingy dress. "Don't cry, Mama. Look what God got us anyway—nothing but sickness and death. The One is the only being I can see who has any control in this world." Mama May gasps at the forbidden name, but Pearl continues.

"Who knows anyway? Maybe The One *is* God."

Chapter 17

"ISN'T SHE SOMETHING?" The One Who Is The One says to the man behind him, his eyes still locked on the small screen. "While others rot from the plague like sewer rats, still The Gift prevails."

The One's young protégé sighs and stalks across the room, his polished soldier's boots echoing on the metal floor. He is tallish, no more than seventeen, and his straight-backed posture and sour, pursed lips hint at a strict upbringing among the very wealthy. His dazzlingly convincing smile and his straight white teeth make him a living poster for the clean, optimistic New Order. With white-blond hair combed severely back from his forehead, pale blue, almost clear eyes, and prominent cheekbones, he seems made of glass—sharp and colorless. Beautiful but hard. Cold. His name is Pearce.

Pearce surveys the rows upon rows of surveillance screens that light up the control tower, showing every corner of the compound. With a tap of his fingertip, The One can incinerate any of the children pictured. He often does so for sport on lazy afternoons.

But The One's attention is focused on a different monitor now — one depicting a scene far across the capital.

Pearce peers over The One's shoulder at the group of filthy-looking individuals passing around candles in a tiny, dank room. The girl is there, The One's precious *chosen one,* standing among them.

Alive.

Pearce follows The One's gaze to the fire roaring in the corner. "It's barely a spark," the soldier says with disdain.

"Ah, but the power of a single spark!" The One smiles, amused. "You didn't find it so easy, as I recall," he notes.

When Pearce remains bitterly silent, The One clears his throat. "I have to say, I'm growing a bit impatient at this point," he says lightly, as if commenting on the weather or the civilian death toll. "Was I not clear when I said I wanted her captured?"

"The squad and the mutts are on their way," Pearce replies with cool confidence.

The One presses his lips together. "Ah. So am I to understand that you employed demonstrably incompetent idiots to do a job that I brought you here *specifically* to do?"

Pearce runs his fingers through his hair in frustration. The trouble is, the thought of getting close to Wisty Allgood stirs intensely conflicting emotions in him — and he is not one accustomed to feeling much emotion at all.

"Couldn't we just kill her?" Pearce suggests. The words

are out before he can stop them. The One raises an eyebrow, and Pearce sees his grave blunder. "It would be easier, faster," he explains quickly. "Without the existence of The Gift, there's no threat. We'll have all the power there is to have."

The One stands up and stares down at Pearce as if seeing him for the first time. His mouth twists into a sour grimace. Then, without a word, The One strikes Pearce hard across the face. The blow makes the boy stumble backward and leaves a deep gash where The One's spiked ring with the New Order insignia has caught Pearce's high, chiseled cheekbone.

Blood is dripping onto the floor in bright, vivid exclamations, but Pearce doesn't cry out, and his jaw is still hard, defiant. After all, in his short life he's been dealt much worse.

"You've developed a bit of a stutter, my boy. I think you mean *I'll* have the power, don't you?" The One says evenly. "And I don't see much of a threat, really. More like an interesting little game we're all playing."

Then The One turns away from Pearce dismissively and goes back to gazing at the screen. Pearce feels a familiar fury heat up his cheeks and his ears, moving all the way down into his fingertips.

There is only one person in the world whom he hates more than the witch.

The young soldier reaches a tentative hand toward The One. If he is strong enough, if he has it in him, he will have no better opportunity. An inch or two more, and he can touch that smooth, bald head, watch the skin peel away from the skull and the body collapse.

Hand shaking, he hesitates.

The One whirls around, and at the same time Pearce jerks upward, as if choked by an invisible vise.

"Getting a little ahead of ourselves, aren't we?" The One laughs maniacally. "Gunning for 'game over' already?"

Pearce's legs dangle as he's suspended inches above the floor, and his face quickly grows crimson and bloated. "You wouldn't," he sputters.

The One's Technicolor eyes dance with wickedness as he holds Pearce aloft by an invisible noose. "As you know too well, dear boy, there is virtually nothing I wouldn't do to educate those who don't completely understand my authority."

Pearce looks past The One and thinks he can just make out the white-topped mountains in the distance, mocking him. The Wizard King's domain. He never should have left.

Just as he is losing consciousness, Pearce falls abruptly to the floor in a pitiful heap.

"Now," The One says softly, leaning over him. "Bring. Me. The. Girl." His smoldering eyes flash a warning. "Please."

Pearce's breath comes in jagged gasps as he struggles to his feet. Regaining his composure, he salutes, turns sharply, and strides as confidently as he can manage toward the door.

"And, Pearce?" The One says when the youth is almost

out of the room. Pearce stops in the doorway, his nerves buzzing. "Remember who made you what you are. If you want to go back to the mountains, I can take away every ounce of power I gave you."

Pearce's body goes rigid, but he doesn't turn around. He touches his cheek and finds it still wet with blood. Biting his tongue to keep from screaming, he straightens, wipes his hand on the doorknob, and goes out to find Wisty Allgood.

Chapter 18

Whit

I'M A WANTED fugitive, a criminal of the highest order whose face is plastered on every wall, every lamppost in the capital. Considering how insane things are right now, getting up at five in the morning, tramping through a city crawling with soldiers, using a big chunk of my M to conspicuously morph my arm into an ax, and hacking down a tree in the middle of Overland Park on a banned Holiday is probably one of the riskiest, stupidest things I could do.

It's not even a great tree. It's a little sparse around the back, and it leans dramatically to the left, but seeing the look on my sister's face as she and Pearl drape scraggly tinsel over its branches makes the trip totally worth it.

Pearl hasn't said much to me yet, but her eyes are shining with emotion.

She looks at Wisty and nods her chin in the direction of the fireplace.

"Pretty good fire you've got burning there. Been going for almost two days now."

Wisty grins—coming from Pearl, this is high praise. I want to join in their moment, but at the mention of the fire, I've got that charred corpse in my head again. I feel nauseated.

Wisty catches my expression and looks perplexed. As much as I want to tell her about what I witnessed in that alley, more than anything I just want to forget it and get my sister far away from the capital.

Wisty, on the other hand, wants to draw out this Holiday for as long as possible.

She winks at me and Pearl, and in a moment the broken ornaments, sitting crudely on the branches, transform into a rainbow of winking electrical lights, the colors glowing in the dark room.

I whistle in appreciation, and the other Needermans gather around, the kids oohing and aahing.

I smile at Pearl, but her tiny face is a mask.

Mama May coughs. "Pearl Marie, honey, where are your manners? What do you say?"

Pearl's big gray eyes are solemn. "It's great, really pretty and all. It's beautiful." She looks at both of us accusingly. "But if you're who they say you are, if you've come to save us, can't you do something *more*?"

"Pearl," Mama cuts in, anger creeping into her voice. "I'm sorry, Wisty, she's just upset. With Ziggy's death and all—"

"Yeah, Mama, they've given us some twinkly orna-ments. But I worked hard for those pieces of broken glass. What has *she* ever worked for?" Wisty stares at the floor, and I put an arm around her shoulders. "And the Feast Day was terrific. But we're going to be hungry again tomorrow, and the day after that. Can they keep this whole family warm at night? Warm and safe?" Pearl asks. "*Every* night?"

No one says a word; every sound has been sucked out of the room. Pearl Marie's eyes are burning into us, hold-ing us accountable.

Right then there's an earsplitting explosion of splinter-ing wood, and the door caves in. A dizzying number of Death Squad recruits flood into the space, their black boots like rats scurrying over one another, their weapons trained on the space between our eyes.

I was almost getting too comfortable for a second there. *This* is more like my life.

I look around frantically for a weapon or a way out of this situation, but there are too many soldiers and too many guns and too many snarling, biting wolves, their mangy coats reeking of rotting flesh, bloodlust in their eyes.

There's a moment of silence, and nobody moves. It's like the Death Squad didn't really expect that it would be so easy. We are animals caught in a trap, staring into the face of our demise. Where can we go? My mind races with my pulse, and I sense my sister next to me, tensed, ready to spring on my cue.

Pearl looks mesmerized by the wolves, her small body

literally shaking. "Stick with Mama May," I whisper. "Don't look back, just *go!*"

"Under the direct order of The One Who Is The One," a chubby recruit reads from a ledger, "the members of this household are to be placed under arrest for the despicable deeds of harboring high-risk fugitives and practicing those forbidden acts and readings associated with what was formerly known as the Holiday, punishable by execution in Orderly Square."

The Needermans seem resigned through their tears. They knew this day would come.

"Nice tree," one soldier says flatly, sneering. "Sturdy wood, pine. Should work nicely for your hanging gallows."

They lunge forward, and chaos erupts. The Needermans seem to have disappeared, and in their place is a frenzied group of scattering mice. Some of the soldiers are stomping at the floor, and one phobic guy is shrieking in fear.

Wisty winks at me, and in an instant I'm reminded that when it comes to morphing things, rodents are her specialty.

In the pandemonium, we're able to dart past the soldiers and up the crumbling staircase to the destroyed apartments above, hell's beasts snapping at our heels. Frantic, dizzy, we circle up and up. I haven't considered what we'll do when we reach the top when the staircase just...ends. The next floor is bombed out, and the only thing that stands between us and the bloody, snarling jaws of the wolves is a shattered window.

One of the men laughs as his wolf strains against the chains. "End of the line. Where else are you gonna go?"

"Now would be the time for a hawk spell," I say to Wisty.

This is when we'd typically morph smoothly into graceful winged creatures, taking flight and soaring above this red-bannered city, our pursuers nothing but tiny black smudges on the landscape below.

Yet here we still are. Human.

Wisty sighs in frustration. "My power's shorting out or something. It's like it works on other people but not on us."

Without a spell, without a choice, I tackle Wisty and together we tumble out of the fourth-story window, falling, falling...

And then a crushing *thud*.

Chapter 19

Wisty

WHIT AND I stand up, coughing, panting, and a little bruised but victorious.

I glance, bewildered, at the enormous pile of trash that broke our fall, and an old woman nods at me as she walks away down the demolished street, trying to look inconspicuous. A small sign of support and unity. We are not the only ones still battling this unjust system. The soldiers lean out the window, bellowing insults, but they can't get to us.

So why are these N.O. men grinning? I squint up at the window. They've got something small and angry squirming between them.

They've got Pearl Marie.

She struggles against them, her little face fierce with determination, but the men laugh, yanking her arms back and forth.

"You forgot your little pet," one jeers at us. "We could

toss her down to you" — he dangles Pearl out the window as she screams — "but I think we'll just hang on to her for now. You know, for safekeeping."

"You didn't change her, too?" Whit whispers angrily at me.

"I thought I changed them all," I say, irritated. "There's no way I could've missed her!"

"She must've slipped out before then." Whit sighs. "She was terrified of those wolves. I *told* her to stick with Mama May and run. We'll have to find her after we've got our energy back and built up the Resistance forces."

He turns, and I look up to see Pearl's distraught face at the crumbling window, struggling against the pull of her captors.

"We're not just going to *leave* her," I demand. I can't believe what I'm hearing. Back in the days of the Resistance, we never would've left someone behind.

"What choice do we have?" Whit asks, his voice strained with emotion. "You know I care about that kid, Wist. It isn't safe here for you . . . for *us*. I just got you back, and I'm not ready to lose you again."

Whit looks up at little Pearl Marie. "We'll come back for you!" he yells. "We promise. And we always keep our promises." I catch sight of her brave nod as the guards sweep her away — and swiftly down the stairwell, I'm assuming, toward us.

Resentfully, I dash down the alley of rubble after my brother, mice fleeing in our path. After we've been running for what seems like forever, I turn to Whit, still angry. "That's not true, what you said," I tell him.

He looks at me, confused. "What's not true? I didn't say anything."

"That stuff you told Pearl Marie when we ran away like cowards, when we left her there at the mercy of those goons," I say bitterly. "You said we always keep our promises. Who have we made promises to, Whit? Celia. The Resistance kids. Mom and Dad."

Whit's face flushes, but he remains silent.

"A big help we've been to all of them, big brother. We shouldn't be making promises to anybody, not to a single soul, and especially not to that doomed little girl."

Chapter 20

Wisty

"GOT...TO...STOP. Going...to...barf," I wheeze.

I slow to a halt next to a closed fast-food joint, and my brother, who's way ahead, jogs back to me. It's almost nightfall, and we're not even out of the capital, but the plague has weakened me more than I want to admit.

There's a huge neon sign blinking the One-Der Burger's logo: THE ONE IS FOREVER. CONSUME HAPPILY. I'm doubled over, but I turn to cough some phlegm in its direction.

Whit's eyes are full of concern. "You okay, sis? I'm fine stopping for the night. You're looking a little wrecked."

I shake my head. "I'll be okay. I just need to catch my breath. It'd be nice if we could just fly or something."

"Your M still acting up?" Whit's frowning at me.

I roll my eyes. "I know, okay? It was dumb to waste all that energy on a weak fire and Holiday lights so soon after being sick, and now my mojo's weak, and blah, blah, blah..."

"No, that's not what I mean. I don't think it's the plague messing with your magic. It's happening to me now, too, and I had trouble with spells before, when you were still unconscious. It's the...air...out here or something that's blocking it."

"Huh," I say, sitting down on the curb next to an appallingly expensive black car, its seats littered with One-Der Burger wrappers. "So we're in the middle of a capital crawling with Death Squad soldiers, The One Who Is The One has a price on our heads, and *neither* of us has any magic to help us out of this mess? Didn't you just whip up a whole Holiday feast and, like, cut down a tree with your *arm*?"

I mime a chopping action and accidentally hit the black car. The alarm goes off, its plaintive wail cutting into the still night air. My adrenaline surges, and we sprint over to hide behind the One-Der Burger Dumpster, but there's not a soul around to respond, and soon the repetitive howl cuts off.

Whit shoots me an annoyed look and steps out from behind the Dumpster. Then he jumps right back into our conversation. "I felt strong in the Needermans' basement, and I was okay if I stayed relatively close, but the farther away we get from that positive energy...it's like a switch has been flipped and I'm about as powerful as a mosquito."

"Looks like our only chance is to get our power from other people," I say.

"What do you mean?" Whit's looking at me like I just read his mind, and he's not super comfortable with it. The blinking light from the One-Der Burger sign gives his face an eerie hue.

"Strength in numbers, right?" I touch Whit's arm, thinking aloud. "The only thing that beats One is two, and three, and four. You said we'd go back for Pearl once we built up the Resistance forces again. I vote we try to find Janine, Emmet, Sasha, Jamilla — everyone we can track down — to help out."

Whit shakes his head like he's about to deliver some really bad news. "They're all on the missing-persons list. Hewitt showed me a copy he'd somehow gotten hold of."

"So?" I challenge. I sound angrier than I mean to.

"So, that means there's no Resistance anymore." He's rubbing his forehead like he does when he's frustrated and upset. He looks me in the eyes, measuring his words. "It means they're probably all dead, Wist. We're all that's left."

My brother's trying to control his emotion, to keep his face strong. To anyone else he'd look calm, resigned. But I'm his sister, and I can hear that slight quiver in his voice; I can see the small twitch of muscles around his mouth. He's remembering them.

I know he's thinking of Janine and the way she took charge of the Resistance with unending compassion and capability after Margo was killed, sending in more and more rescue teams to get captured kids out of the prisons, even as the bombs rained down. Or maybe he's remembering the look she used to give him, the intimate, adoring gaze that he pretended never to notice but that we all could see as plain as day. He'd been the only one who could crack her shell. But maybe the New Order finally broke her.

Like me, Whit's probably thinking of Sasha with his dark curly hair, stubborn and strong-willed but with more revolutionary fight in him than anyone. Or of kind, level-headed Emmet, the gentle giant who my brother knew would always have my back if he wasn't around, who said I looked awesome, even when I hacked off all my hair to stay off the radar.

I cross my arms and walk a couple of paces, thinking of my lost friends and feeling the bubble of grief well up and lodge itself in my throat.

Then I turn around. We owe them more than this. More than just letting them go.

"The One controls that list, right?" I ask. Whit nods. I'm anxious, talking faster and pacing the parking lot even though I'm dead tired from running all day. "Well, just because *he* doesn't know where they are doesn't mean they're not still alive."

Whit's brow crinkles as he considers this possibility. His face struggles between hope and defeat. "But if The One can't find them, how are we going to? They could be anywhere by now."

I think for a minute. "The last time we saw Emmet and Janine was in that underground steam pipe after Garfun-kel's was blown up, before we got separated, right?" Whit shrugs, but I see the doubt on his face. "So we start looking by going back there. Maybe they turned it into the new Resistance HQ."

It's not likely, but it's possible, right?

"All right, Captain Wisteria. If you say we'll find 'em, I guess we'll find 'em." Whit punches me playfully, but I know he's trying to downplay just how much this outcome matters. "Vive la Résistance!" He does an energetic lap around the parking lot, ready to sprint to the steam pipe right now.

"Only, Whit?" I call after him.

"Yeah?"

"I'm not quite ready for another all-night journey through the lion's den of the New Order just yet. I think I'll take you up on that offer to find someplace to sleep first."

Whit bangs on the side of the Dumpster. The mealy, gag-inducing stench of rotting meat is wafting over. *Oh no. I am* so *not going to*—

"Got a better idea?" my know-it-all brother asks.

He plants his hand and vaults his legs over in a graceful move even I have to admire. Whit has always been athletic, but in the weeks we were apart, he must've been training on his own nonstop. He's gotten, as Celia would say, "seriously ripped."

I scramble in after him. As much as I don't want to lay my head to rest among the scraps of the New Order citizenry's garbage, it's strangely fitting, actually. Kinda poetic.

It's also sheltered. And out of the way. And, as my brother has already discovered, full of food. Well, if you can call "food" a quarter pound of deep-fried meat that consists of the body parts of hundreds of different animals and is now discarded in a crumpled bag in the bottom of a Dumpster.

Whit sees my expression and shrugs. "I'm starving," he says, chomping off a chunk of a half-eaten One-Der Biggie Burger. Three words: *Dis. Gust. Ing.*

My stomach complains loudly and Whit grins, holding the bag out to me. "Happy Holiday," my brother says, mouth full. Reluctantly I reach into the sack.

But the only thing left in this bag is a kid's plastic action figure of The One, bald head shining in the weak light of the Dumpster.

My temper simmers, and I melt The One down to nothing in my hand.

"Whoa," says Whit. "You've got some mojo in you after all."

I shake my head. "That's not mojo. That's just pure hatred."

Chapter 21

Whit

"WHIT, BABY? CAN you hear me?"

I wake—or think I wake—to the sweetest voice I've ever heard.

Her face—her perfect, beautiful face—is just inches from mine, and I swear, if my heart stopped beating right now, I'd die happy. Her long dark curls frame her face, and she's looking into my eyes in that calm, unself-conscious way that always did me in. I hold my breath and inhale her scent.

If this is a dream, I never want to wake up.

"Celes, is that really you? I *so* want it to be you." Chasing Celia's image has gotten me into trouble before, and Wisty's convinced it's The One trying to manipulate me. If so, I have to admit, he's using the right angle. Celia's the one thing I can't say no to. I'd probably run into a snarling pile of zombie wolves if she asked me to.

Celia surveys the Dumpster. "Nice digs you got here,

baby. A little fancier than the Shadowland, I'll give you that, but I have to say, you smell worse than a herd of Lost Ones." She wriggles her nose in mock disgust.

I grin. *That's my girl.*

I reach out to touch her face, her smooth, soft skin, and she turns her cheek, mimes kissing my hand even though it's only air. My heart aches. She's never felt more real, but moments like this don't last very long.

"Oh! I almost forgot!" Celia reaches into her pocket. "I brought you a present for the Holiday," she says, and smiles in that way of hers—shyly—that brings back a rush of memories so potent I almost can't take it: the first time she placed her hand in mine, her slender fingers so warm; her face when I scored the winning touchdown; the day she first introduced me as her boyfriend; the first time I saw her, as a ghost, after she disappeared.

She places the object in my hand, and I can actually feel it. It's a fountain pen—sleek, shiny, perfectly crafted—just like Celia. I've never used one of these, but I can't wait to try it.

"Celia, it's…this is beautiful," I say, turning over the pen in my hands.

She smiles, pleased. "It's not as old-school as it seems. Really. You can write with it anywhere, on any surface, and it'll record your words wherever you want. You can write your story, no matter where The One forces you to run."

"I'll write your story, too," I vow.

But suddenly Celia's eyes look far away, like she's reading from a letter. "And, Whit? There's something else I have for you. A message. From your parents."

My heart seizes up. If my parents can still contact us through Celia, if we can still communicate, it's as if they're not really gone. "My parents? You've seen them?" I manage.

"Your dad said to remind you: You and Wisty need to share your Gifts if you're going to get anywhere. And your mom said to be brave, and not to be afraid to let go." Celia smiles sadly. "But you and I both know you're not very good at letting go, right, baby?"

The air around her is cold, way colder than it should be.

She's leaving. She's always leaving.

I jerk awake and bump my head against the metal of the Dumpster. My hand, still reaching for Celia, is thrown over the side and is freezing in the night air.

Hopelessness floods through me. I love her so freaking much—but what's the use in loving someone so fiercely who is dead?

I'm clutching something in my other hand, clutching it for dear life.

The pen.

I must've created it from the dream. Apparently I've got some M left after all.

Chapter 22

Whit

"WHIT, WAIT *UP*," Wisty whines.

We're on the outskirts of the City of Progress, and I'm barreling ahead of my sister on streets where New Order–confiscated middle-class homes jockey for space among abandoned, dilapidated buildings. I know neither Wisty nor I got the best night's sleep behind One-Der Barfer, but sometimes when an idea strikes you just gotta move on it.

There are few armed soldiers this far out, but I can still hear the shrill howls of dogs scrabbling in the distance. Dogs that have been trained on our scent. Mobs probably lurking in every alleyway, eager to burn us to ashes. We have to keep moving, and now that I have a destination in mind, I want to get there as soon as possible.

Wisty jogs to catch up. "I thought we agreed we were going to head to the steam pipe. You're going the wrong way."

"I know, but I was thinking we'd take a little detour

first." Wisty stops and crosses her arms, and I clear my throat. "A short trip to the clinic where you volunteered with those sick kids, for example?"

Wisty doesn't say anything. She's probably thinking of her still-healing scabs and the terrifying fever-induced delusions she endured when she *almost died* just a few days ago.

I don't blame her. It's just that I can't get that "message from our parents," from Celia, out of my head, even if it was all a dream. "Don't kill me! Listen, when I used my M to heal you, I felt this amazing relief to have you back, but there was something else, too. It felt *right,* like healing was exactly what my magic was meant for."

"Hmm." She leans against a rusting chain-link fence and examines the blister on her heel. She looks up, eyebrows raised, impatient.

"Then I had this crazy dream, and...I'm just starting to get this feeling that we should be doing more, and if I can help a few sick kids to get better and grow up to keep fighting against The One, that doesn't seem like such a bad thing."

I expect Wisty to protest at least a little, but she nods thoughtfully. "Yeah. After what Pearl said about fulfilling the Prophecy, I've been thinking about what we can do to help, too. I do want to find the Resistance members if there's a chance. But the steam-pipe area is likely toxic, heavily guarded, or both. Who knows? Maybe someone at the clinic has heard something about our friends."

"Great," I say, relieved. "Let's get going, then, slow-poke." I take off.

"Whit?" Wisty calls after me.

"Yeah?"

"It's in the other direction."

Chapter 23

Whit

AS WE NEAR the center, it's like I can feel the power within me growing. Seeing all of these people in need in one place seems to help reopen the channels of magic that The One's influence has shut down. I look to my sister, and I don't even have to ask.

"I feel it, too," she says. "I think I might even have enough juice to do a morph. Might be safer."

Disguised as middle-aged hospital staff, we head into the clinic, which is in an old parking garage from the days before the New Order restricted vehicle use for officials only. Wisty's rocking a blond perm and a fake tan, and I look like the once popular comedian Mark Dark, all scruff and slouch. I make a mental note to keep up my workout routine into my forties. The paunch is *not* working for me.

Inside it's way worse than I expected, and apparently a whole lot worse than when Wisty was last here. For one, it's all kids.

Moaning, bleeding, dying kids. Kids on filthy cots or sprawled on mats on the floor among the decades-old auto grease.

Wisty gasps, her hand covering her mouth. We've seen a lot under this brutal regime, but this is ... too much.

"It's The One Who Is The One's latest 'cleansing program,'" a nurse says from behind us. Her face is lined with worry, and she looks like she hasn't slept in weeks. "Or at least that's what the rumor is. The New Order wants to expand its fancy headquarters into the old town, and the youth in that district seem especially tough to convert. So if the cleansing can take out a few thousand young potential dissenters in the process, that's just icing on the cake."

I want to hit someone. That's not accurate. I don't want to hit just anyone. Just *One* person. I want to bash his bald head in.

"Let's get on with it," Wisty says bitterly, and I know she's just trying to keep it together. She still knows her way around the clinic and heads to the end with the youngest kids, where the floor starts to slant up to the next level.

A young nurse named Lenora whom Wisty recognizes nods to us as we gather bandages. We help her move a few of the delirious kids from the floor to free cots. They feel like tiny birds in my arms, hearts racing.

"There's never enough beds," Lenora huffs, wiping the sweat from her freckled forehead. "We try to keep the sickest off the floor, but the plague seems to be mutating." She unwraps a toddler's soiled, unsightly dressings and uses fresh gauze to cover the sores, cooing to him as he cries. "Before, some had a chance, the fighters could pull through. Now, it takes almost every single one, and quickly. These children aren't in good shape, but those over there are faring the worst. If you can stomach it, what they could really use is someone to hold their hands. All any of them wants is a mother."

We walk over to where she's pointing. It's darker, and quieter. The kids don't talk or cry in this part of the garage; there's only the sound of labored, shallow breathing. Wisty is pressing her lips together, her face pale. I know she'd hold every single kid's hand as he died if it would help, but I'm hoping we can do better than that.

The first patient we visit is a little boy with sallow skin and the telltale plague scabs on his face. His big brown eyes are still lucid as they peer at us, but they're shot with red. He doesn't say anything as I put my hands on his shoulders, just sucks his thumb and squeezes his eyes shut against the pain.

I don't want to think about what has happened to his mother.

I nod to my sister, and she places her hands over mine. For a moment nothing happens, and worry fills my chest, but then I feel the jolt of energy as our power surges into this boy. We watch in awe as his breathing evens out and the red drains from his eyes.

"I can't believe that actually worked." Wisty gapes.

I shrug self-consciously. But then the boy smiles up at me, and I feel...like God.

Wisty and I get a sort of assembly line of healing going, and while we're not able to save everyone—some of them are too far gone—in just a short while we've got half the clinic on the way to better.

Each healing process takes a lot out of me, and I can feel my energy draining, but when I put my hands on these kids' frail shoulders and feel the M flow into them, it's nothing short of incredible. My fingertips heat up, and my heart, and I feel this surge of—I can't explain it. Light, energy, warmth. *Love.*

It's seriously addicting.

Wisty and I are just about to focus our energy on an eight-year-old girl emaciated with sickness when my sister looks up as if coming out of a trance. "Wisty!" I say, irritated. We have to keep going if we want to get to everyone. But I stop when I see her face. She looks like she's seen a ghost.

"Is that..." Wisty squints, striding across the dimly lit space. She beckons me over toward the far end, where there are an alarming number of recently vacated cots waiting to be cleaned. My sister is standing over a thin, dark-skinned girl who looks around seventeen.

"Whit, I think it's *Jamilla.*"

Chapter 24

Wisty

"IT CAN'T BE her," my brother whispers.

It's obvious what he means. The Jamilla we knew, our old friend from the Resistance and the house shaman back at Garfunkel's, was cheerful, vibrant, and easily more than two hundred pounds. This poor plague victim has been stripped of all hope and is so emaciated by the sickness that I'm not sure her bones can even support her.

I look into the sick girl's face, at her sunken cheeks and mottled skin. I recognize her corkscrew hair. Her eyes, though bloodshot, still have the depth I remember.

She's a ghost of her former self, but it's Jamilla, all right.

"Jamilla," I whisper. Her eyes drift over us, unfocused.

"We're still all morphed out," Whit reminds me. "She probably doesn't recognize us."

I bend over her. "Jamilla, can you hear me? It's us—Whit and Wisty."

"You!" she says hoarsely, fear creeping into her eyes. "It's *you!*"

Whit looks at me uneasily.

"Yeah, it's us," I say, trying to sound reassuring. "We're not going to hurt you. We're here to help you." She whimpers, and I want to comfort her. She's scared, really scared.

Scared of *us.*

But Jamilla's tormented mind can't stay focused on us for long. Her eyes roll back and she's delirious again, mumbling about the "plague of the poor" and moaning names I recognize: Sasha. Janine. Emmet.

I want to ask about Emmet especially, since we'd been pretty close, but there's a change in the mood of the place that's putting me on edge. Minutes ago the kids we'd healed were lying in peace, contentedly beginning their recovery. Now, many of them have struggled out of bed and are huddled together, whispering. They have a look of utter terror in their eyes, like the Grim Reaper himself has come with his scythe to rip them from safety.

"It's Pearce, for sure," a healthier boy says gravely as he sneaks back up from the first level. The whispers are replaced by harsh silence as this sinks in.

"What're they saying?" Whit asks, straining to listen to their whispers.

"No. No, not him, not—," Jamilla whimpers. Her breathing speeds up until she's hyperventilating. "Get out!" she rasps. I don't know if she's talking to us or them.

Whit puts a cool cloth on her head, trying to calm her down as I peek around the corner to see what is making everyone panic: two New Order soldiers are stalking among the cots with the air of hyenas circling an injured calf.

Whit and I are disguised, but my breath still quickens. There's something about the way dozens of kids are reacting to these two that makes my skin crawl. These aren't just the normal drones we see every day in the streets practicing their swagger; these men are corporate.

The soldiers seem to be doing a routine inspection of some sort, working their way across the room with a clipboard. A woman—the nurse who first greeted us—is following behind them, nervously twisting her shirt in her hands. No one else moves, and the air is heavy with the smell of fear.

One of them can't be much older than my brother, but he has a distinct air of authority about him. He's tall, with white-blond hair and sharp, angular features, and I'm weirdly drawn to him. He'd be really attractive if something about him didn't seem so soulless.

A broad, almost garish smile plays across his face as he joins us on the second level and takes in the hordes of near-death children, and when his piercing blue eyes settle on mine, it's as if ice water is flooding my veins.

I catch Whit's eye. This morph isn't going to last forever, and I sure as heck don't want to be in a claustrophobic obstacle course of a room crawling with cops when I return to my usual, conspicuously redheaded self.

I start to pack up supplies as Whit whispers healing words to Jamilla, but sucking the plague out of so many kids has taken a lot out of him already, and I can see that his M is weak.

The soldiers are selecting beds to be wheeled into an armored truck.

"No!" the nurse protests as they begin to cart away a weak little girl who has already started to heal. She wails, and tears spring to the nurse's eyes. "Have you no heart? These people are sick, *dying*. You can't just snatch them up like rats to run your 'tests' on!"

"The One Who Is The One demands compliance." The soldier with the clipboard cocks an eyebrow, his young face alight with cruelty. "Unless you'd like to go in her place?"

The nurse steps back, terrified, and the soldier laughs, high-pitched and haunting, and I'm reminded again of the hyena. "Thought not."

Jamilla moans in pain.

"Whit," I plead, "can't you *do* something? We're losing her." Whit places his hands gently on her shoulders again and concentrates.

"It's no use." He sighs heavily after a minute. "She's too far gone."

The soldiers are getting closer, and our time is almost up.

"Jamilla," I beg the dying girl. No response. "I know you can hang in there. You're going to get out of here and see everyone you love again. Emmet, Janine..."

Her eyes snap open and bore into mine with terrifying intensity. She's clutching at my arm with every bit of strength left in her frail body. "Janine...," she croaks, "Janine is...lost..."

"What do you mean, *lost?*" Whit asks harshly, and I bite my lip.

"Whit, don't. Just let her be —"

"*Lost* as in *dead?*" His voice cracks.

"Lost...," Jamilla whispers, and then her grip on my arm slackens and her eyes flutter closed. I can't believe this is happening. Another tragedy.

Whit shakes her shoulders, and I wince. "What do you mean? Where's Janine? Come on —"

I swear my hands are starting to look younger, paler, and soon my fiery hair will be falling around my shoulders. Not now. Please, not now.

"Whit, we have to go."

And then I feel the blond soldier's cold, calm smile on me. It's almost flirtatious, and I'm stunned by desire, then shame. But before I can sort out these strange emotions, Whit grabs my arm and we're running, running, running, again.

Chapter 25

Wisty

"JANINE," MY BROTHER huffs between breaths as we run near the icy gray harbor. "What Jamilla said. *Lost.* Can't let her down..." He sprints ahead. "Gotta...find her."

We're finally headed for the steam pipe to see if we can gather clues about what might have happened to Janine and the rest of the Resistance kids, regardless of the risks. We've run through the now-inactive war zone where our old headquarters at Garfunkel's used to be, past the bombed-out holes and craters scarring the streets. We're nearly to the manhole that leads down to where we last saw our friends.

But when I see the angry, frustrated look on Whit's face as he slows to a stop, my stomach knots up around my heart and I can't help but imagine the worst.

But the reality is even worse than that.

Cold horror stops me in my tracks as I spot a crowd in the clearing, poking and jeering at two teenage girls tied to wooden posts. Stacks and stacks of kindling are piled at their feet.

They're about to burn them alive.

"Please, we don't—," the one with the longer hair pleads, sobs choking through her words. "I swear, we're not even real witches." At this word the crowd goes wild, surging forward with sneers and screams. The girl wails in desperation.

The other girl is maybe two or three years younger, and her small face is unmoving—hopeless and dead, like she can't really fathom that this could be happening.

My stomach twists and heaves. I can't believe it either.

The two are sisters, by the look of it, their dark almond eyes and thin noses mirror images of each other. With their whimsical, eclectic clothing—now torn—they stand out from the crisp red suits of their tormentors, which must've made them targets.

"Not again," my brother whispers at my side, tearing me back from the scene.

"You've...you've seen something like this before?" I say, anger and disbelief creeping into my voice. My accusation is clear: How could he not tell me about something so serious?

"I know," Whit says. His face is pained, apologetic. "That's why I was so freaked back at the Needermans'. Why we had to leave like that...even with Pearl..." He trails off, and I remember her flailing in the soldiers' arms. "I was scared, Wist. *Really* scared. I just wanted to save you from all that."

"*Save* me?" My voice is rising. "How is keeping me in the dark—?"

"I couldn't do anything last time anyway!" Whit snaps. "I was too late." He sighs heavily, his eyes on the ground. "Never mind that, okay? These girls don't have much time. What are we going to do about it?"

He's right. We can't sit back and watch this. I look at the crowd. It really isn't that big, just totally nuts. We could take them easily.

"How about we show them a *real* witch burning?" I suggest with a raised eyebrow.

Whit nods grimly. "I like your style, sister."

And with that, I'm off and running, crazy like I haven't been in weeks or months... heading full-speed at the unsuspecting crowd, windmilling my arms, shrieking bloody murder. Of course, flames are leaping from my head in a macabre halo of fury, too.

At first the mob comes together, undulating toward me and buzzing with possibility. But as I get closer, the people begin to scatter, the whites of their eyes bulging in terror, convinced that their day of reckoning has arrived and that this apparition will make them pay for their crimes. That's pretty much exactly what I was going for.

Cowards at heart, every one of them. They want to burn every imaginative kid in sight, anyone who is a little bit different and therefore vulnerable. A real witch is, of course, too much for them.

As I lurch at the frenzied masses, my fire roaring, Whit

rushes to the girls and works at untying their binds. In minutes we have them freed and the square cleared of the murderous bigots.

After it's over, the sisters cling to each other, mute and dazed from shock. They're shaking violently.

Whit fingers their open gashes where the ropes cut into their flesh, healing them, but they flinch even at his touch.

"It's okay. You're okay," I whisper, rubbing their shoulders. "It's over. We're here to help. Can you tell us your names?"

"I'm Dana, and she's Lisa," the older girl says. "I don't know what happened. We were just walking. I had this hairpin...a woman yanked it out of my hair and then they were all around us, pushing and shoving, scratching us with the pin, saying our blood was poison..." I can see she's usually the chatty one, but right now her voice shakes and it's clear she's trying not to totally lose it. "The thing is, we're not really even witches." She hiccups. "Not like you." She winces, fidgeting awkwardly. "I mean—"

"It's okay." I smile. "I like being a witch."

"I just like to cook weird things, and Lisa plays the ukulele. I know it's illegal, but"—tears spill onto her cheeks—"we never thought those things would get us killed."

Lisa, the younger one, has doe eyes, huge and frightened beneath her fringe of heavy bangs, and they keep darting back to the ominous woodpile behind us. She squeezes Dana's hand, comforting her sister, but her body remains tensed as if ready to sprint. If only she knew where to run to, where it might be safe.

"You guys can come with us," I offer. "We're trying to find our friends and get the Resistance back together." I see Lisa's eyes jump longingly in her young face. She looks at Dana, the question hanging between them. But Dana shakes her head.

"No." She sighs. "We really need to get home."

I nod, the idea of home feeling sweet and sad. Home is long gone for us.

The sisters shuffle off into the gray streets of our fallen city, arms wrapped around each other, shaking after their ordeal.

I snap my fingers and watch as they transform into squirrels, scampering inconspicuously along the park's edge. It'll wear off within a couple of hours, but it should get them home without trouble, if they can avoid the poor scavengers in the alleys looking for a meal.

"Safe travels," I whisper.

Chapter 26

Wisty

WE START TO head in the other direction down the road, but it looks like word of our little rescue has already gotten out. There's another, different group of people headed toward us, and I can tell even from here that they're official N.O. Our middle-aged-staff disguises have fallen away, and we're exposed.

"Here we go," Whit says beside me.

As they get closer, I see it's the young blond soldier from the clinic. And he's not alone. He's got around two dozen comrades with him this time, and they're all freaking *giants*. Not just big-boned but, like, seven and a half feet tall, all decked out in way-too-tight N.O. T-shirts that emphasize their gigundo muscles.

My eyes flick to the bank of the harbor. We could hop the fence, dive in, still have a chance at a getaway. It's maybe ten running steps to the fence, and I'm faster than any of these big boys, guaranteed.

Whit sees me looking at the water and shakes his head. He's reading my mind again, and now I'm reading his: He's saying, *We'll take what comes, Wisty.*

"Well, look what we have here," the blond soldier says, his quiet voice velvety and menacing at once. He's still smiling that pearly, patronizing smile, his wolfish demeanor incredibly sinister.

I suspect we just might find out why all those kids were so afraid. He can't be much older than I am, but he's already got that cold, calculating look of a man driven by greed.

"So this is the famous Wisteria and Whitford Allgood, the deadly witch and wizard," the soldier says with mock enthusiasm. "We hear that you've ruined a perfectly good barbecue. It is my great honor to meet you, despite all the...messes...you've been making." His eyes sparkle as if we're all in on the joke.

Talking is always my first form of defense, and my motormouth starts right up before I even know what I'm saying to Blondie. "I'm sorry we can't say the same about you and your extra-large playmates," I blurt.

It doesn't come out as confident-sounding as I'd hoped, because the truth is, I'm seriously creeped out by this guy. There's just something about him that seems...psychopathic. Unpredictable. Like he could kiss you or cut off your limbs and he'd probably feel the same level of excitement.

The soldier laughs, and it makes me shiver. "They said you were funny. Isn't she funny, guys?"

The giants move in around us, roughly wrenching our arms behind our backs.

"And such lovely red hair. Like flame," the leader says, stepping toward me. He strokes strands around my face, and I flinch. My cheeks heat up in a mix of embarrassment and vanity. I can feel Whit tense beside me.

"Regardless, The One Who Is The One will be most pleased that you're on your way to see him," the creep continues. "In fact, I'm happy to personally deliver you. No extra charge for the service. You have my word on it." He smiles again.

"I think you're going to have to break your promise on this one," Whit says tightly. "My sister and I aren't going anywhere with you, buddy."

"Pearce," the soldier says, extending a pale, well-manicured hand. "My name is Pearce."

Chapter 27

Whit

PEARCE CHUCKLES, WITHDRAWING his hand. "So sorry. I see you're otherwise occupied."

I try to twist away from this jerk's beefy sidekicks, who are still holding us back. I'm already wound pretty tight, and another obstacle isn't helping. The narrow strip of asphalt where we're standing along the water is about the only area that hasn't been demolished around the old Resistance stronghold, and it's impossible to look at the craters in the wounded earth and not think of our friends. If they're alive — and that's a big *if* — they're definitely running out of time.

And now we have to deal with this egomaniacal kid. "At ease, boys," he says, and they instantly free our arms. Pearce looks like a child next to these seven-foot goons, but they're clearly afraid of him. I get the feeling he shouldn't be underestimated.

"So *this* is the famous healer, the incomparable athlete,

the sensitive poet." Pearce steps forward and peers into my face as if he's studying an intensely interesting scientific specimen. How does he know all of this about me? We might be in it deeper than I thought.

I stand up straighter, my bulk and height an implied threat. If Pearce thinks I'm going to shrink away from him, he can think again.

"And it's a shame we don't have time for you to give us a bit of a show, Wisteria," he muses, turning to my sister. The way he says it—suggesting things that are much more uncomfortable for an older brother to imagine than just a fire show—makes my hands ball into fists. I take a step in front of Wisty, and Pearce smirks at me. "Dynacompetents are so very rare these days," he says mildly.

"And so tricky to catch," one of the giants mutters from behind him.

Pearce's head whips around to glare at the loudmouth. Touchy subject apparently.

"Did we not discuss this beforehand, Fafner?" he asks the giant, venom dripping from his words. This is obviously a guy who is used to having things done his way. "That you were to be *silent* while I was interacting with the Allgoods?"

The underling ducks his head and says meekly, "Yes, sir." A circle widens around him as his buddies move off, condemning the offender.

"Come here," Pearce says almost inaudibly.

Fafner is shaking now, cowering, and Wisty looks at

me sidelong, unsure of what to expect. "But I didn't mean—"

"I said *come here!*" Pearce explodes. He wraps his black cloak tightly around him as the wind coming off the water ripples his fair hair, and for the first time I notice the goose bumps on my own arms.

Reluctantly, Fafner slinks toward Pearce like a dog with its tail between its legs. When the man's close enough, Pearce reaches up and touches the giant's head, as if he's blessing him or something.

And then the most insane thing happens: the skin on the giant's face seems to just... *fall away*. All that's left is a naked skull sitting atop this huge body, and when Pearce lets go, the body crumples to the ground.

Its skull rolls to a stop in front of us.

As Wisty and I stand there with our eyes bugging out of our heads and our mouths hanging open in disbelief, a few of the other big boys drag the body toward the bank, and Pearce wipes his hand nonchalantly on a handkerchief.

"Where were we?" he says, turning back to us and smiling brightly as if nothing's happened. "Ah, yes, you were about to accompany me to visit The One."

I am scared. I am horrified. I am super freaked out at this guy's total lack of self-restraint, and a little in awe of his power. But I'm furious, too. Livid. This is not the world we were promised as children, and no one is ever going to make this man pay if I don't right now.

"What, you can't handle us yourself?" I taunt. I know

the way egos work—you just have to push the right buttons. "You're probably nothing without that pathetic little trick of yours. I bet I could take you, mano a mano."

I normally don't sink to this base level, I swear, but I'm just about at the end of my rope, and there's no way I'm letting them take me in without a fight. Today, I let Celia slip through my fingers again. Today, I watched a good friend die. Today, I found out Janine—calm, compassionate, serious-eyed Janine, whom I care about more than I want to admit—is probably dead. I'm ready to pound someone into the ground, and if anyone ever deserved it, it's Pearce.

"Oh, come now, Whitford. Must we always resort to violence?" Pearce ironically raises a conspiratorial eyebrow at me as if reading my thoughts.

I flex my fingers in response, and then he starts to laugh—deep, rolling peals of laughter that are incredibly unsettling coming out of that stern, cruel face. The rest of us stand around awkwardly, not really sure what's so hilarious, but Pearce just keeps right on cackling. The guy is seriously unhinged.

"*Mano a mano*," he snorts. "How about *mojo a mojo?*" And then out of that wide, gaping mouth of his bursts a powerful gust of wind.

Next thing I know I'm on the ground, coughing, confused, and breathless, my feet knocked clear out from under me. He blew me right over. Like I was a blade of grass.

As I'm trying to get my breath back, Pearce's face becomes serious.

"Your M doesn't work so well in the city anymore, does it, Golden Boy?" he purrs. "Unfortunately for you, mine does."

Chapter 28

Wisty

"WHIT!" I YELL, struggling against the three big goons who've now got my arms wrenched behind my back.

My brother holds up a hand, telling me to chill, like he's got this whole nightmarish scene under control, but he's on his knees, already down. Blood from his nose is making awful, bright patterns on the asphalt.

Whit can't expect me to just stand here and watch as Pearce does his face-melting trick on him, too, can he? After I've already watched my parents die, and my friend Margo, and countless innocent kids, now I'm just supposed to do *nothing* as my brother takes on this complete sociopath?

Pearce smirks at me with the look of a person who enjoys torturing small animals, and something in me snaps. Now that the glamour has worn off, my M is coming back. My fingers start to tingle, my face gets hot, my temper boils over, and then...

I . . . just . . . explode.

The guys holding me drop my arms, wincing as if they've been singed, and suddenly there are three-foot flames reaching out from my body, white-hot and roaring.

I start to move toward Pearce, my wall of fire reaching for him, but he doesn't budge.

He doesn't even look frightened.

Unfortunately, before I can scorch anyone in a blaze of glory, I'm tackled by at least ten of the seven-footers, who proceed to stop, drop, and roll all over me.

So much for the New Order freak roast.

Chapter 29

Whit

"BRAVO. BRAV-O!"

Pearce claps slowly in mock appreciation. He's licking his lips and circling Wisty closely, that predatory smile playing across his face.

"I must say, Wisteria," he taunts, his lips nearly brushing her ear, "if I didn't hate you so much, I might be in love."

Wisty scowls, and I lurch at him. I'm immediately restrained by the giants. "If you even *touch* her, I'll—"

Pearce's icy eyes twinkle with amusement. "You'll... what? Write a poem about it?"

"Absolutely. It'll be called 'Ode to a Smashed Face,'" I quip lamely, trying to hide my alarm.

"Ah, yes. 'Mano a mano,'" Pearce says mockingly, making air quotes with his hands, then pauses. "What do you say, Whitford, still up for a little fight to the death?"

"Uh...," I stall. A breeze wafts in the smell of the seawater behind us, but I can think only of the giant's skull grinning up from the bottom of the harbor, and it makes me queasy.

Wisty shoots me a look of alarm and disapproval. This is so *not* what we're into, but I feel backed into a corner here. And, though I'm ashamed to admit it, there's a tiny, dark, sick part of me that wonders if I could actually do it.

I nod at Pearce uneasily.

"Whit!" Wisty protests, and I try to convey *What else am I supposed to do?* with my eyes. I glance around at the eerie setting—the demolished buildings, the abandoned path, the waves crashing against the shore again and again like they have for millions of years. Apart from homeless plague sufferers squatting in the doorways of half-fallen buildings, there's no one around. No one else to bear witness. No one to hear me beg for mercy.

Maybe I can just knock him unconscious long enough to get out of here.

"Brilliant. Rency...?" Pearce looks behind him.

The biggest goon of the bunch steps forward and nods, cracking his knuckles, and I swallow hard. *He can't mean...*

"Wait, are you *serious*? I meant *you* against *me,* Pearce. What kind of coward has a guy twice his size fight in his place?"

"Oh, this isn't about courage at all, Whit. It's much bigger than that. I'm interested in seeing what you can do. A test, if you will. As in, to see if you can *not die.*"

Chapter 30

Whit

THE GIANT AND I circle each other, my mind racing to come up with a *not die* plan.

The truth is, the odds aren't exactly in my favor.

I'm a pretty solid guy, and I've gone toe to toe with many a gargantuan thug during football (often called *fool-ball*, the way we played it, since it was such an insane version of the sport). But Rency is built like a bulldozer, with his veins popping out of his thick arms like ropes. Even when he crouches down, I barely come up to his chest.

Rency has a glint in his eye, and he looks around at his bros, who all start laughing, and a knot forms in the pit of my stomach.

It's quickly replaced by a sucker punch from the giant that leaves me gagging and doubled over.

Then a knee explodes into my chin, a clublike fist spins me around like a top, and a metallic taste fills my mouth.

Through double vision I can just barely make out my sister's anguished face.

Pearce looks disappointed on the sidelines, as if he's about to lose a bet.

Then something happens that I can't quite explain. Something clicks, and a knowledge, an understanding, a *power,* is unleashed within me.

I slide forward as if following some secret choreography, jab my left fist like a thunderbolt to connect with Rency's chin, cross for a body sack with my right hand, then spin out of the giant's reach.

Jab, cross, left hook, pivot, low jab, spin, *wham!* My body moves without my direction, anticipating the man's every move and applying advanced hand-to-hand-combat techniques I'm sure I know nothing about. As my fists connect with his jaw, then his temple, then his kidney, it's like I'm standing outside myself.

I feel furious. I feel powerful. I feel *invincible.*

I feel... out of control.

My arms are incredible deadly weapons of steel that Rency doesn't have a fighting chance to fend off. His face is practically roadkill, and his left arm is hanging at a weird angle from his body, but I can't stop.

As my boardlike hand connects with the giant's kneecap, I'm relieved as Rency finally goes down like a rock, his face distorting into a mask of pain.

He's not dead, but it's over. I look down at my fists, unable to comprehend what just happened.

Pearce steps into the circle. "Loser." He scowls, putting his hand on Rency's mammoth square head, and the giant crumples, the two empty eye sockets of his skull gaping up at us.

My stomach churns. I am *never* going to get used to that.

"Well done, wizard," Pearce says, the jovial tone returning to his voice. I tense, understanding the underlying threat. "That was certainly an entertaining little act you put on for us. Unfortunately for you, your sister is the only Allgood The One really needs. Since she is The One With The Gift, you are...what's the word? Expendable."

Pearce bounds, catlike, and before I can direct my newfound defenses his way, his deadly hands are gripping the sides of my head, searing into my temples.

The world burns bright, then shatters.

Life rearranges itself into just two words, flashing in bold, blinking letters across my consciousness: *stop* and *pain*.

It's...excruciating. My eyes roll back but snap open to punctuate each new bolt of agony pulsing through my body. I see: one of Pearce's icy blue eyes, squinting; the top of a tree, its bare branches clawing at the dismal sky; Wisty's slender fingers across her mouth, holding back a scream; a white-hot, blinding light.

My brain is a fried egg that can't seem to process anything, a short-circuiting mass of nerves screaming for this experience to end.

But it goes on. And on. And on. *Why isn't it over yet?*

My vision comes into focus again just long enough for

me to see the shocked look on Pearce's face, and then his features harden with determination again.

He leans forward and squeezes my skull even harder. My jaw is clenched tight enough to grind steel. I grasp at his fingers, frantically trying to rip them free, and I feel my legs buckle, my knees smashing into the hard ground. I wonder vaguely if other bodily functions have given way as well, but it's a fleeting thought as my entire being is immersed in another explosion of anguish.

I have a hazy understanding that that awful sound—that shrieking, that brutal, animalistic howl echoing off the buildings and drowning out the waves from the harbor—must be coming from me.

How am I still alive?

With this realization, this glimmer of hope, I focus through the physical pain, somehow numb my senses, and concentrate every effort on shutting out the energy flowing into me, pushing away the blinding light, healing. But still the pain throbs, and I'm done for, I can feel it, the life leaking out of me, my systems shutting down, when...

Abruptly it stops. The pain. The dying. All of it.

Pearce screams, clutching his head as I had only moments before, and staggers backward, collapsing onto the ground in a dead faint.

At that instant, nausea overtakes me, and I spend a moment retching on the ground, black spots dancing in front of my eyes. When I can see straight again, I wipe off my mouth and sit up, trying to focus on my surroundings.

The giants are edging away from me with baffled, horrified looks on their faces, and my sister's mouth hangs open, her expression a mixture of shock, concern, and victory. Tears are streaming down her face.

I'm nursing the worst migraine in the history of headaches, but I've still got enough brain matter left to understand this simple fact: for maybe the first time ever, Pearce's skull trick didn't work.

What does that mean? I wonder, right before I black out.

Chapter 31

Wisty

"WHIT? ARE YOU alive? Whit!" I'm shaking my brother's shoulders violently, trying not to get hysterical while I'm alone with a dozen bewildered giants and two passed-out wizards. *Whit's fine*, I tell myself. He looked okay, or relatively okay, right before his eyes rolled up into his head.

Wake up, wake up, wake up, I urge silently. *Wake up before Pearce does.*

I eye the handsome psychopath sprawled on the gravel. His hard features look softer, almost gentle, in his unconscious state.

Whether as a result of my telepathic begging or not, my totally ridiculous, irresponsible, admittedly awesome older brother finally stirs, his eyes fluttering open. I don't know whether to hug him or smack him, but he's not registering my shock/awe/relief anyway. He's preoccupied with something else.

"Is that—?" He squints, looking past me.

I turn to see Mrs. Highsmith, our parents' longtime friend, standing just behind me, looking grand in an extravagant hat and an impeccable bloodred silk suit.

The last time I saw her she was pressed up against her ceiling, being tortured by The One until her eyes bulged out of her head. Yet somehow I'm not surprised to see her now — she's that kind of lady.

"You silly children! Out here *without proper coats!*" she scolds, seemingly unaware that Whit's covered in blood, there's an unconscious guy on the ground next to him, and we're surrounded by confused, brawny bouncers. Is the dotty-old-witch persona an act? I have no idea; she likes to keep us guessing. "What would your mother think? And I'm supposed to be looking after you!"

She hasn't exactly consistently lived up to that task so far in our sad tale, but I have to admit, she's gotten us out of a couple of jams with some surprisingly powerful M, and I'd bet she's got another few tricks up her designer sleeve. You know those teachers you think are totally kooky and weird but whom you actually learn the most from in the end? Well, I'm hoping that's how this turns out.

Mrs. H. glances over at Pearce, who seems to be regaining consciousness. "Tsk-tsk," she clucks. "I knew that one was a bad apple from the start. What a temper! I expect he'll be a bit crabby when he wakes up, hmm?"

She squeezes our hands, turns abruptly, and commands, "Better *run!*" We stumble after her, but even in heels the old witch is way faster than we are.

Chapter 32

Wisty

MOMENTS LATER, WE'RE sitting in Mrs. Highsmith's new kitchen in her new apartment, since her last apartment basically had a tornado hit it—a tornado courtesy of The One Who Is The One.

Where exactly is her new place, you ask? I'm not quite sure, but from a glance out the window, I'd say if she's trying to blend in with the New Order drones, she's doing a good job.

How did we get here? I can't exactly tell you that either. All I know is that Mrs. H. took off ahead of us, the world seemed to cave in on itself, the laws of physics reconfigured, I felt totally motion-sick, and the next thing I knew, I was sitting on a barstool and Mrs. H. was asking me to pass the witch hazel.

I feel like I've been playing with a light socket, and Whit's fuse looks seriously blown, but when I glance up at Mrs. H., not a hair is out of place on her gray head, her suit remains perfectly pressed, and she's still clicking around in those impossibly high heels.

Typical.

Mrs. H. is stirring a brew of the foulest-smelling business you can possibly imagine — like a marriage of sulfur and sewage that is going to produce some truly rank offspring. I back away from the stinky slop and join Whit in taking in the surroundings.

Her new apartment isn't homey and welcoming like her last place was; I guess to live among the N.O. elite, you sacrifice space and personality. She's got a red-clad doorman and a depressing but striking view of the Capitol building from her fifteenth-floor window.

She has kept some of the key things from her last place, though, and they don't exactly add to the feeling of roominess. The walls are crowded with banned art, and sculptures lean in doorways, just like I remembered. There are pathways carved out through the litter, but so many musical instruments cover the floor anyway that someone's going to break an ankle. The woman has some real hoarding issues.

And books. Stacks and stacks of books, everywhere. Jockeying for space on bureau tops, tipping over on coffee tables, piled in swaying mountains on the floor. Even if I didn't get straight As, I always loved to read, and now that just about every single book has been *banned,* the pull is even stronger. I feel almost tender toward these tomes. The

One has taken away our power to learn, grow, imagine, and escape through words.

Why didn't we fight harder to keep it before it was torn away?

I pick up one book gingerly and brush off its dusty cover.

"*The Cemetery Book*," Mrs. H. says over my shoulder. "Terrific choice. Plenty of great wisdom in that one."

"Yeah, like what?" I laugh. "How to avoid dying? Because that's some advice I could actually use."

"Well, yes, and that you shouldn't fear the dead," she says, looking at my brother eerily. "The dead, like all of us, have ... limitations."

She says it in that weird voice she uses to convey Greater Knowledge. I roll my eyes. Mom would probably smack me, since she said Mrs. Highsmith was here to help us, and anyone who can duke it out with The One Who Is The One and hold her own (or at least not get killed on the spot) is one tough witch. Still, can I just say how sick I am of adults doing the wink-and-nod charade, like, *Not until you're older?* I mean, we're supposed to be the children of the Prophecy who change everything. Any advanced knowledge would be pretty freaking helpful right about now.

She turns to me. "And, Wisteria, you would do well to remember that wits, courage, and compassion are the keys to survival." Her eyes sweep the room, sparkling. "And music."

I nod. Now *that* I can relate to.

On Mrs. H.'s command, rock music pours into the apartment, and she starts to shake and sway, the beat taking over her muscles. She stirs the pot as she moves, the gruel sloshing over the sides.

"I remember every song I've ever heard, every note!" Mrs. H. shouts over the music. Then she frowns. "Well, almost every song. Of course, there are notable exceptions. Anything by the Cumin Girls I sort of *choose* to forget, for instance."

When a familiar old ballad blasts through the room, I join in.

"Oh yeah!" I shriek. "Turn it up!" I look around, but I can't seem to locate where the music is coming from.

Mrs. H. shoots us a shy smile and taps her ears, and the volume increases. "Never forget, lovelies, the music comes from within."

I shake my head at the old adage, but I have to smile. She's a fruity old witch, that's for sure, but she's right. She's always been right. Suddenly I'm filled with the same feeling I had just once before, when performing onstage in front of thousands of Resistance supporters at the Stockwood Music Festival, amped by a wall of speakers created with my own magic. I shiver. One day I'll get back there.

Maybe Mrs. Highsmith and I have more in common than I thought.

My brother takes her hand and whips her around the kitchen like they're at some kind of ball. After a minute she turns to stir the soup, and Whit grabs my arm, laughing. We spin round and round to the familiar tune, and when we finish in a dip, laughing, Whit's eyes are shining.

"That was Dad's favorite song," he says, breathless.

"Yeah." I sigh, eyeing one of Mrs. H.'s guitars longingly. "I really wish that he'd lived to see me rock the socks off the New Order."

"Had lived?" Mrs. Highsmith raises an eyebrow. "Oh, children, you didn't *really* believe they were dead, did you?"

Tears well in my eyes instantaneously. The hoods. The crowd. The smoke.

The awful smoke.

"What do you mean?" I demand. "Are you claiming they're . . . alive?"

"Well, they're alive for now," the old witch says. "Barely alive. Alive, as in struggling to breathe air in and out. As yet unextinguished, if you will."

"Wisty, don't believe her," Whit says, jaw set. "I saw it with my own eyes. I watched them get . . . *executed*."

Mrs. Highsmith laughs her musical laugh, and it looks like Whit might actually strangle her.

"But, darlings," she says lightly, gesturing toward the shiny surface of the cooking pot, "see for yourselves."

My brother hangs back, unbelieving, but I'm unable to stop myself from bolting forward. At first I can't see through the salty tears, but I rub at my eyes, and there, on the lid, are two bent figures with sunken eyes and hollow cheeks, standing near water.

Mom and Dad.

Alive!

Chapter 33

Whit

A LITTLE CRY escapes Wisty's mouth, and I rush forward to join my sister.

My parents seem to be standing near a river, waiting with a lot of other people. They are emaciated and as pale as paper.

"Mom!" I shout. "Dad!" Their faces waver like an image caught in steam.

Wisty looks at me, her eyes pleading. "What are they doing there? Those don't look like New Order soldiers—"

"Dad, where's the river? Tell us where you are!" He doesn't answer, so I turn to Mrs. H. "Is it in the capital? Do you know how to get there?"

"How do we find you?" Wisty asks, her hands gripping the sides of the lid.

Mrs. Highsmith's kind eyes look at Wisty, then at me. "The river is in the Shadowland, of course," she says gently.

"Where else would it be, lambs? That's where the river has always been, where people cross over to the other side."

I grab Wisty's arm, ignoring Mrs. H.'s ethereal BS for the moment. "We can get there. We just have to find a portal to the Shadowland, and we can bring them back. I don't care about the risks, I don't even...Wist?" She isn't listening to me, and I follow her eyes back to the image of our parents and see why.

Mom's eyes are looking right into hers, and she's shaking her head in terror. "Stay away!" her lips mouth at us in her gaunt face. "Promise not to come here!" she wails. "You. Must. Not. Come."

Dad steps behind her and puts one hand in the air like a stop sign. He looks about a hundred years old, and the gesture seems to zap the last of his energy, but his eyes are fierce as they lock with mine. "I forbid it," he says, and suddenly I feel tiny, like I'm four years old again and asking to ride our neighbor's bike. Dad's eyes blaze inside his gray face, and just when I'm about to cry out to him, my parents disappear.

"No!" I shout. "Wait!" But the image has vanished completely, and the lid reflects my own horrified face in its place.

Wisty's voice comes out in a whisper. "They're alive. And they want us to just do *nothing*?" I can see she's close to losing it.

"Mrs. Highsmith"—I turn to the old witch, suddenly angry at her for not giving us the guidance she'd promised—"you think I care what they said about staying away? We're obviously going there. Will you help us find the portal, or are we on our own?"

Mrs. H. looks like she's got a million other secrets she'll never reveal. "There will come a time in your lives, Whitford and Wisteria, when you have to make your own decisions, when you have to go your own way, when you have to disobey the injunctions of your parents." She peers into our faces, eyes bright.

"I'm thrilled you understand that that time is now."

Chapter 34

Wisty

"NOW EAT UP, children, I've a plan."

Mrs. H. puts two steaming bowls of the gruel in front of us. It looks and smells like cat food, but whatever. Whit eats a spoonful and then pushes the rest of the bowl away while trying not to make a puke face. I think I'll pass on mine. We're not here for the food anyway.

"Listen very closely, dears. If not followed explicitly, this plan could easily result in your deaths."

Well. At least she's being straight with us.

"Whitford, I understand that you have experience in the depths of the Shadowland." Whit nods, and Mrs. H.'s eyes bore into him.

"Look ahead. Your vision will serve you well, young man, as you journey to this foul place of writhing, hungry spirits. The labyrinth will deceive you, but you must navigate the depths of the soul to find your parents. Follow the animals to the river, and love will meet you there."

Whatever *that* means.

Whit looks like he doesn't totally speak Mrs. H.'s language of soul riddles, but he nods solemnly anyway.

I, on the other hand, am already getting annoyed. Our parents are out there in some Shadowland abyss, and I'm sorry, but I don't have time to learn about the meaning of life before we find them.

Still, when Mrs. H. turns to me, I find I'm holding my breath. "And you, Wisteria, have the greatest task of all. I'm afraid your trip will be arduous, your task mammoth, and the odds overwhelmingly stacked against you."

She pauses meaningfully, and I lean forward. "Anything," I say. "I'll do it." Now that I know they're alive, every fiber of my being aches to see Mom and Dad.

Mrs. H. beams at me. "It is you, and you alone, who must deal with The One Who Is The One. Now."

Wait, *what?* My spoon clatters to the floor. The One, as in the all-powerful One who's been trying to track us down and skewer us for months?

"You're not serious." I stare at her in horror, my jaw hanging open like a guppy's.

Mrs. H. nods expectantly.

"Our parents are on the verge of *death*, here," I protest, incredulous. "And while Whit gets to go traipsing after them in the Shadowland—which I have experience in, too, by the way—I'm supposed to just...what? Knock on the door of the most powerful being in the Overworld and then...'*deal with*' him?" I'm shouting now.

Mrs. Highsmith looks me over with quiet disapproval, and then she says something totally whackjob: "Tell me, Wisteria, do you remember anything, anything at all, from your Biology 101 class? How about physics? Chemistry? No? I should have expected as much from a truant."

I shudder involuntarily at the familiar words. It's practically the *exact* same thing The One said to me back at his pad, forever-and-a-day ago, when I was supposed to be proving myself as a witch. Mrs. Highsmith cocks an eyebrow, and I'm speechless.

Just what exactly is going on here?

I glare at her. "Look, if you want to focus on the past, fine. In the past, we've seen The One control water and air and the earth. We've watched him empty oceans, whip up tornadoes, and split open the ground with a flick of his pinky finger. How is *anyone* supposed to fight that?"

Mrs. H. nods and holds my face in her hands, and I feel like I'm about five years old. "But what he doesn't have is your fire, Wisty, your energy, your *electricity*. He may control the earth, but he doesn't control the people on it. At least not in their thoughts. Not yet. But if what The One believes is true, if your powers extend to the electrical impulses of the brain, he'll *use* you to control not only the government of the Overworld but the actual *minds* of all humanity, in every dimension."

I frown, uncertain what to make of this. Whit's kneading his knuckles into his forehead, deep in thought.

"Don't you understand the implications of your power, darling? If The One Who Is The One succeeds, it will be the end of the last shred of free will any of us has left. It will be the end of resistance, of creativity, even hope. It will be the end of ... *everything*."

"Okay." I sigh, feeling like a very heavy chain has just been placed around my neck. "But what am I actually supposed to *do* to beat The One? My so-called Gift feels like this thing that's so much bigger than me, something I can't even totally control, and I'm not even sure what it's for."

Mrs. H. considers her answer. "The Gift is certainly not to be used to *be* God. Only to prevent others from trying to be God." I nod, waiting for a directive, but Mrs. H. shakes her head. "I can't tell you exactly how to use these tremendous Gifts you've been given," she says gravely. "To grow and to understand the Prophecy, you must learn to master them on your own."

I sigh, the gravity of this situation settling in my gut.

I'm supposed to infiltrate a heavily guarded compound and pick a fight with the most powerful being the world has ever seen, and Whit is supposed to go stumbling through the Shadowland, where people either are eaten by the voracious Lost Ones or get so lost in the haze that their minds turn to gruel. All because of a Prophecy someone saw written on a wall. Because, for some reason, they all believe in us, a truant and a foolball star.

I look at Whit, the one person I can always count on, who has been with me through every terrible loss, every struggle, every victory. *Are we really going to do this?*

Whit nods, his eyes bright with hope, and I squeeze his hand, suppressing a feeling of panic. *Of course we are.*

Besides our lives, what else have we got to lose?

BOOK TWO

A FEAST OF SOULS

Chapter 35

Whit

THE SHADOWLAND IS a labyrinth of despair.

It's a knot of wrong turns, a blanket of fog weakening your resolve, a stench of lost souls who'll do anything to claw their way out of this purgatory. The Shadowland is the taste of fear in your mouth urging you forward, deeper into the maze, farther from any connection to time, sanity, or the living.

But the Shadowland is also Celia, the girl I loved and lost, a beautiful soul known in this purgatory as a *Halflight,* whose life was taken too early, whom I'd do anything to get back. And now it's my parents, waiting for me by a river in the depths of its secrets.

So, with a cocktail of emotions coursing through me, I'm finally on my way there.

But first I have to get to the portal—the only one Mrs. H. is sure is still in operation. It's deep in an area of the capital I've never been through before. I walk briskly, and soon the elegant white stone buildings give way to a concrete no-man's-land full of heavily guarded factories belching thick, white steam into the still air.

I turn down a narrow alleyway, and shadows shift as men bundled in rags move away from me in the dark. I stand straighter, trying to make the most of my big frame.

I walk beside the concrete wall, barbed wire snarling along the top, twelve feet up. A red sign tacked to it reads TESTING FACILITY—KEEP OUT. Two exhausted-looking soldiers are keeping watch, but one appears more concerned with rolling a cigarette. The security measures almost seem ridiculous anyway; the rumors of what goes on in The One's experimental labs are more than enough to keep out the curious.

Except vengeful wizards, I guess.

Though these guys seem like slackers, I see the brass N.O.P.E. pin of honor on the soldiers' uniforms, meaning that they're actually commandos in the New Order Portal Elite squad (the existence of which the N.O. vehemently denies, of course). They're Curves, drafted to enter the Underworld and report back, since The One is officially a Straight and Narrow who can't travel between the worlds himself.

Trained wolves snarl at the N.O.P.E. soldiers' feet, teeth bared and ready to snap.

I picture my parents' wan faces, Dad's forbidding hand, and the fear in Mom's eyes. Something was going on there at the river, something they didn't want me to see. But nothing—not Dad, not The One, not even a pack of wolves—is going to keep me from the Shadowland.

It's the last place in the universe any sane person would want to be, but that terrifying land of stolen memory and shortened lives holds Celia, my parents, and everything I've lost.

For better or worse, the Shadowland holds my destiny.

Chapter 36

Whit

WHEN YOU'RE BACKED into a corner, sometimes the only thing to do is the stupidest thing you can think of.

To that effect, without so much as a disguise to help me out, I march up to the New Order thugs slouching against the dirty concrete. "Confidence is key," Dad always used to say. "You can do almost anything if you believe you can."

And, actually, it kind of works for a second. I don't betray any motive, and it's as if the guards have forgotten that they're supposed to be *guarding* the place. They just look at me with bored expressions. For a minute I think I'm actually going to get away with strolling right past them, but unfortunately the wolves are a bit more on the ball.

The death dogs snarl and start to tug at their chains, mouths foaming at me in hunger and hatred. This perks the soldiers right up, and they scramble to get their weapons pointed at me.

The youngest one tries to be authoritative. "No one

136

goes in or out, bub," he says, his gun leveled between my eyes. "Entry is strictly forbidden."

"I've been sent by The One Who Is The One," I hear my voice telling them calmly before I know what I'm saying. The older, bald one looks at me uncertainly and mutters something to his comrade, and I try not to let my hands shake in front of the hell beasts, who probably have built-in lie detectors or something. "I have an official letter," I continue boldly.

One of the guards nods and holds out a hand expectantly. Great. I do not, in fact, have an official letter. All I have is a crumpled-up slip of paper with Mrs. Highsmith's directions to the portal on it, but I pull the pathetic thing out of my pocket anyway and thrust it at him.

The older one takes the proffered letter and unfolds it, then barks, "What's this? It's just a piece of paper with street names. Arrest—"

Before the guy can get the rest of the words out, I'm off. *This* is what I've trained for. *This* is what I was made for— saving my parents. My feet fly beneath me, faster than I've ever run before, carrying me straight at that heavy wooden door guarding the portal.

And as I hear the wolves snapping at my heels, as I sense the guards taking aim with their fingers quivering on the triggers, I hope, I pray, that I'm still a Curve, that my body will bend into the other dimension, that I'll melt through this solid door into the Shadowland and into the arms of Celia, and my parents, and everyone who is counting on me to be a hero this last time. I'm praying that I don't just smash into that oak and get arrested.

Because after all I've been through, after all Mom and Dad have been through, that would seriously suck.

I'm flying, leaping, flailing forward with one final heave, holding my breath, and the last thing I feel is a tremendous *crack* as if my head's exploding.

Chapter 37

Whit

WELL, THAT WAS…intense.

With portals, each one is a different experience, but it's never very much fun. There have been times it wasn't unlike going through a car wash; times it felt like being "squeezed out a birth canal" (in Wisty's words); and one notable episode when I was sure I looked like a tomato smashed against a wall when I came out the other side.

But this one was unlike anything I'd ever gone through. After that initial nasty bump on the head, I thought it was all over, but then I felt the weirdest sensation, like my cells were rearranging themselves or something.

I'm definitely in the Shadowland now, because I can hardly see a thing.

"Celia!" I call out tentatively. "Mom? Dad?"

As I stumble through an opaque wall of fog, I gag on the smell of rotting sewage—no, rotting *flesh*—and my heart flutters with recognition.

Lost Ones.

Less-than-angelic humans stuck in the labyrinth of the Shadowland so long their very souls have rotted into a mass of stink and decay. Monsters tormented by loss and demented with hunger.

Hunger for human flesh.

God, no.

I hear the screams of men being tortured, *devoured.* Soldiers? The N.O.P.E. guards, leaping after me into the portal and into the cannibalistic maws of Lost Ones? I shudder violently, but though the shrieks go silent, there's nowhere to run.

Suddenly dozens of decaying arms grab at me from out of the smoke, their slimy flesh slipping around my shoulders, my chest, my throat. I scream, but the sound is muffled among the moaning and frenzy.

I push back at them, wrenching my body in utter terror.

"Don't try to fight us, idiot," a low, garbled female voice coos into my ear, full of ill intent. "You can't win. Don't you see? We're already dead." The others cackle, and the Lost Girl continues. "Don't you wish you were dead?" She puts a clammy hand on my cheek, and I recoil. I'm glad that I can't see her rotting face through the haze. "You will be."

She laughs, and my stomach turns as I now begin to make out a hint of stringy flesh left on her face as it shakes terribly, her cavernous eyes dancing in front of me. "Soon. Very, very soon, you'll be dead, too, handsome idiot stranger."

Chapter 38

Wisty

MY FACE IS scrubbed clean, my hair is brushed, glossy, and trailing down my back like a flame, and I'm decked out in a chic green dress that Mrs. Highsmith had lying around. I click along the spotless streets in my too-tight shoes as if I don't even care that the security cameras from the surrounding mansions—each of which I'm sure comes equipped with a vicious wolf-mutt growling just beyond the gate—are trained on my every move. If it weren't for the glint in my eye, you'd swear I was New Order Youth all the way.

After weeks on the run covered in blood, grime, and who knows what else, I almost feel like I'm going to a fancy N.O. recital. My old frenemy Byron Swain once told me about those so-called parties that culminate in an elaborate recitation of The One's successes, with the N.O. elite dressed to the nines and patting one another on the back. As excruciating as that would be, I wish I were going there—instead of where I'm actually headed....

My showdown with The One, maybe to save the fate of the world, but more likely to die.

I'm muttering Mrs. Highsmith's advice—"wits, courage, compassion"—like a mantra, and I'm so worked up I almost walk right in the path of a Youth Troop on patrol.

There are two straight lines of stone-faced children, marching stiffly in crisp white uniforms accented with bold red trim. The leaders are just kids—probably younger than I am, but they've got the cold, brainwashed look of soldiers of the highest rank. Not one of them would hesitate to bash my head in.

They've got a few even younger kids with them, who are being dragged along, sobbing, in chains.

New Order families and couples stroll by, elegant in their fine clothes. They don't look at the chained kids, or seem to hear their wails.

But I do see the looks on those kids' faces, the hopelessness and the pain. I *do* hear their screaming. I walk past the banner-lined street that will take me to the palace and The One's headquarters. Without even meaning to, I find myself approaching the troop instead. Though it's the last thing in the world I want to do, I can't *not* help.

Chapter 39

Wisty

I HAVE THE sudden, eerie feeling that something is horribly wrong as I'm walking toward the troop. I can almost feel hands pressing down on me, choking out the air, and even in the thin material of my dress in the chilly breeze, I start to sweat.

Whit is in serious trouble.

How can I help him now? Entrances to the Shadowland are few and far between these days, and I could never get to Mrs. Highsmith's portal quickly enough. The Youth Troop is standing at attention; they've already spotted me ambling toward them. *I'll just have to pray he can get himself out of whatever horrible mess he's in,* I think, remembering Rency's ruined face.

I'm on edge, and the cold stares of the troop as I approach aren't helping. What kind of moron walks right up to brainwashed killers without even so much as a disguise?

Yours truly.

I panic and do a quick face-scramble, but the New Order Youth start to crack up as I draw near. They point and snicker, imitating me, and I get the sinking sense that maybe I'm a little cross-eyed. And that my nose is skewed to one side of my face.

The kid at the head of the line blows a whistle sharply, demanding decorum. I can't see his face, but the troop immediately stands at attention.

"Just kidding around," I say, forcing a weak laugh and quickly rearranging my features. I tap the last kid in line on the shoulder, and he spins around, ignoring the reproach of the whistle-blower up front.

"I'm, um... I'm here to join the troop. I want to be a New Order soldier someday," I gush. "I was hoping to... destroy freedom and imagination...?" Other kids gasp and turn around at my mention of the forbidden words. Perfect.

A boy with jet-black hair snaps the strap of my dress. "Oh really?" he sneers. "You're not exactly up to protocol with this little 'outfit.'"

An older teenage girl yanks on my newly disguised dirty-blond hair. Her own hair is so tight it pulls back her whole face. "And didn't anybody tell you? All the spots for uglies are full."

I shrink inside even though I know the truth: I'm the only one in the world with enough power to rival The

One's. But a well-aimed insult can still sack me with a boatload of self-doubt.

"It's my dream to honor the N.O.," I press on, careful to keep any hint of irony from creeping into my voice. "Truly."

Chapter 40

Wisty

"TRUE NEW ORDER Youth material joined at the beginning of the ascendancy," the girl says as an older boy wrenches my arms behind my back.

"They saw the light of The One Who Is The One. They followed the path of true justice," another boy says with robotic detachment while the first clamps handcuffs around my wrists.

"All others are fakers. Wannabes," a stern little girl with braids chimes in as they march me to the front of the line with the other prisoners. "They are At Risk. They support the unholy cause of the Resistance. They must be stopped!" her shrill voice screeches.

The black-haired boy cuts in, whispering in my ear, "That's where *we* come in. On the direct orders of His Greatness, it's our job to make such heathens"—he snaps his fingers, grinning wickedly—"disappear."

I draw a sharp intake of breath. A Y.E.S. — Youth Extermination Squad! I'd thought they were just a sick rumor.

The boy shoves me into the center of the two lines, and I huddle against a couple of the smallest prisoners, a girl and a boy no older than five, with rivers of tears running down their grubby cheeks.

I hear Mrs. Highsmith's voice in my head. *Confident. Powerful.*

"There's nothing to be afraid of," I whisper to the shivering kids.

Other than torture and death, or maybe just being turned into a mindless drone for the remainder of your days, that is.

"Take me to your leader," I say to the leering New Order Youth sarcastically.

"Oh, come on, Red," a voice says from the front, a voice that knows how much I hate that nickname. "For a girl who so desperately wants to join the N.O., you could put a little more *feeling* into it." I know that nasally accent, that whine.

The boy with the whistle turns around, his eyes scanning my face as if he doesn't recognize me, as if he hadn't been trying to win my heart for ages, as if I hadn't once turned him into a weasel because he was such a freaking traitor. As if we'd never met.

He grabs my arm roughly and marches me along. "Your

wish is my command. To the leader we go. Nice dress, by the way."

The whistle-blowing head of the Y.E.S. is none other than Byron Swain!

Chapter 41

Whit

I'M IN CHAINS, but I can still speak. And as long as I'm alive I won't stop trying to get answers.

"I'm looking for Benjamin and Eliza Allgood. Is there a girl around here named Celia? If you tell me where the river is—the place where people, um...cross over—I can help you get out of here, too. I swear I'll help you!" There's real desperation in my voice, but the Lost Ones are too busy right now to answer my questions.

They're busy doing the same thing they've been doing for hours since we arrived at their camp, or hideout, or whatever this eerie, foul-smelling place happens to be: they're busy eating forest animals.

Live.

I feel bile rising in my throat. I may never eat meat again.

I turn from the grisly scene, but the metallic smell of blood nags at my nostrils. The word *abattoir* pops into my head, dark and foreboding. I can't remember what it means, but it conjures up images of hacksaws and horror shows. Of muscle pulled from bone and the frenzied desperation of animals awaiting slaughter.

The feeling of *I'm next.*

The fog isn't as thick here, and I can make out surrounding forests. I'm trying not to look over there, though, either. The trees are not made of wood and leaves but *bone.* The clouds above are red, menacing, and our shadows seem to have a life of their own; they slither along the ground like snakes, mime acts of violence, dance up your back. I'd run, but there's nowhere to go. Everywhere outside this valley is thick, opaque fog.

We're way deeper into the Shadowland than I've ever been before; I had no idea any of this existed, but maybe it means I'm finally getting somewhere. Where there are forests and clouds, there's got to be a river, right? Mrs. Highsmith said something about following the animals. Could she have meant these sad, torn-to-shreds creatures?

I strain to see through the fog, squint for some hint of water in the distance. No luck, but I do see more Lost Ones. The zombielike creatures shuffle toward the camp, their stench preceding them. They've got something with them being pulled on ropes. Looks like...

Kids?

More kids could mean more chances to dupe these ghouls and escape. I scan the crowd, not recognizing anyone at first—they're still far away. There are several older kids, including a bigger guy around my age; a kid with a bandanna tied around his head; and a couple of small boys. There's an animal with them, too—a big, loping dog that looks an awful lot like Feffer, the Curve dog who once tried to eat Wisty and me before we tamed her.

Wait, it totally is Feffer!

That means these kids are Resistance!

I feel a surge of elation, my pulse quickening.

I want to shout to my allies, but I don't want to set off a frenzy among the Lost Ones. I sit tight, watching the kids file in, impatience making me fidgety. And my eyes fall on a cute girl around sixteen near the end of the line, with wild, curly hair and combat boots.

I know that determined, no-nonsense walk anywhere—

Janine!

Chapter 42

Whit

"WHIT!" JANINE NEARLY plows me over with a fierce hug that takes my breath away. She's tied up, and the other kids grumble as their hands are pulled on the rope, too.

My heart seems to get caught up in my throat. I bury my face in her dark hair and squeeze her with all of my strength. It's a little awkward with the others around watching, but I don't care about anything but this right now. *Thank God she's alive!* Somehow—even in this awful place, captured by soulless creatures—I'm elated.

And surprised to find that the only thing I really want to do... is kiss her.

Janine's never been one for a poker face, and she looks at me with fierce emotion, like she's offering up the whole of herself. "I thought I'd never see you again, Whit! I thought—" She clutches my arms, and my heart beats faster.

"I thought you were dead, too," I admit breathlessly, stroking her cheek.

I still love Celia, and I don't know exactly what I feel for Janine, but I do know that I've missed her more than I thought was physically possible, and I didn't understand that until this minute. Her serious, intelligent face, free of makeup but prettier than any movie star's. Her smart ideas. Her strength. I don't want to ever let her go again.

"Jamilla said...I thought...," I whisper, still over-whelmed. "How did you end up here?"

"The Resistance tried to escape in the Shadowland," she answers. "Whit, we looked for you. We waited and we searched. I didn't want to leave you behind, but the N.O. was *everywhere* in the Overworld, and you and Wisty were on all the posters, so we thought you'd gone into hiding and—"

"Shh...it's okay. We didn't know how to find you guys either. Everything just got so turned around....Are Emmet and Sasha here, too?" I ask, looking around for their famil-iar faces. "Did they make it out?"

Her eyes fill with tears, and she brushes them away angrily. "I don't know. We were split up. I had everything mapped out! We had a plan to get all the kids through to another portal, and Emmet went ahead to scout the path..."

More tears escape, and her cheeks flush in frustration as she continues. "But we got turned around in the fog and just couldn't get away from them." She nods at the Lost Ones. "I've been racking my brains to figure out what their plans are for us. But it's as if they're hungry dogs following a familiar scent home. They've just been hauling us around on these ropes for days, and I think—" Janine flinches uncharacteristically, her eyes widening. "I think they're going to feast on us."

I glance over at the ghouls, still ravaging the bodies of the small animals, and shudder.

"No." I shake my head. "That's not…that *can't* happen, Janine. I won't let—"

Janine shakes her head sadly. "We're too far in. There's no way out." Her sage-green eyes, once so sharp and full of life, seem resigned. "Look, I'm tired of fighting. Can you just…hold me right now, Whit?"

I nod and wrap my arms around her, my chin resting on her cheek, her warm body against mine.

We may not have much time left, but for now we've got this.

Chapter 43

Wisty

MY HAIR IS being yanked, the rope's been tied too tight, and someone keeps kicking me in the heels. As a result of said kicking, I've fallen twice, leaving my left knee bloody and my temper fuming.

Kids trained in torture. I *hate* the New Order.

The Youth Troop, minus Byron Swain—who has disappeared, leaving me absolutely freaking out, once again, about whether he's actually working for *them* or *us*—drags me across the busy courtyard with soldiers practicing endless drills, through three heavily bolted metal doors (reminiscent of my prison days), and finally into the leader's office inside the New Order compound.

"Found this one prowling the streets, General," the snotty girl with the tight ponytail reports, standing at attention. "She wants to join the Youth Troop." She's unable to keep the venom out of her voice. "We thought you could...take care of her."

"Thank you, Genevieve." The general sighs from his chair facing the window, clearly annoyed with the disturbance. He's a large man, with black hair slicked back over his receding hairline. "That will be all."

Genevieve looks disappointed at not being recognized for her achievement, but she nods and follows the others out the door.

The lock clicks into place, and we sit in silence for a few moments, the general still facing the window. I take in the office, every object in it tidy and obsessively arranged. Grubby teddy bears and dolls line the bookshelves like trophies in a taxidermy, and I imagine the small hands those dolls must have been ripped from.

Then, abruptly, the leader spins around and fixes me with a long stare, one of his eyes made of glass and motionless. It's extremely unnerving.

He looks at my mussed-up hair and my bloody knee, and an expression of blatant revulsion distorts his face. "I suppose you have something to say for yourself?"

"I—" I swallow. What do you say to a powerful fascist murderer?

"No matter," he says, striding to the window and thrusting it open. "We don't need to talk. I'm happy to just sit back and take in the sweet sounds of Orderly conduct. Leaps and bounds better than all of that horribly distracting music we used to have around, don't you agree?"

His office window overlooks both the exercise yard, where we can hear the New Order Youth practicing drills, and the detainment area, from which pitiful shrieks and sobs erupt to punctuate the grimness of it all.

I am terrified of this man and his complete lack of empathy. I am terrified of his capacity for torture and his enjoyment of suffering. I am terrified of anyone unperturbed at the prospect of genocide.

But right now I have to be the model of New Order Youth, eager to usher in an age of death and destruction. High on horror.

"Sir, there's been a terrible mistake," I say to his back, my voice animated and full of conviction. "All I want—all I've ever wanted—is to serve the New Order with honor. I approached the Youth Troop because I was stirred by their conviction, but they mistook me for one of those despicable *Resistance* fighters."

He turns around again and fixes me with his fake eye, twisting the ends of his mustache.

"I'll do *anything* to join the N.O., sir. I particularly excel at torture and obeying authority."

The general perches on the edge of his desk and methodically works the tip of a pencil through the eye of a teddy bear. "Save your lies for someone who's interested," he says. "I know exactly who you are, Wisteria Allgood, and you're about to have a very *interesting* last few hours of your life."

I swallow hard, imagining the gruesome acts that can be achieved with a sick mind and a few sharp instruments, but a nagging part of me is wondering how he knew.

Did Byron give me up—*again?*

Chapter 44

Wisty

"IF YOU KNOW who I am"—I try to keep my voice strong, try not to plead—"you know how valuable I am to The One Who Is The One. He's your boss, right? As in, you *answer* to him?" I hate myself for using a man I loathe as a shield, but I feel trapped.

The general doesn't say anything but takes out a slip of blue paper and calmly starts writing.

"If you harm even one hair on my head," I press, "it will dilute my Gift. Maybe even ruin it. You can't hurt me."

"Level-five prisoner," he reads, his pen poised above the paper. "Traitor to the people. Scheduled for confession of her crimes against the New Order." He looks up at me, and his glass eye stares, unwavering. I feel a tight knot of panic in my chest. "Confession to be obtained by *any means necessary.*"

He knows who I am, and he's not afraid. This man

enjoys the screams of small children. Just what exactly might he have planned for *me?*

"You c-c-can't do this," I stammer. "You'll pay for it! When The One finds out what you've done to my Gift, he'll—"

The general's face is a mask, his good eye seeming bored. "And where, pray tell, is this Gift of yours now, Ms. Allgood?"

I start to sweat, and my throat goes dry. He's right. Where's the fireball? Why aren't I flaming out?

Why does my magic keep short-circuiting when I need it most?

I think about what Mrs. Highsmith said about my potential to control electrical impulses in the brain. I don't quite believe it's possible, but The One sure does. And if I ever get out of this office, I'm going to have to take him on. Maybe it's worth finding out if I even *possess* this Gift that he so desperately covets.

I look at the general, his head bent over his desk, and imagine the evil thoughts flitting through that warped brain of his, imagine the unspeakable deeds he has in mind. I imagine those thoughts dissipating...evolving...

I concentrate every ounce of power I can muster into the effort, like a laser beam zeroing in on the head of a pin. Then I feel white-hot electrical energy sparking through my body, and just as I think my brain might explode, the general suddenly looks up from his writing.

"You know, Wisteria," he says seriously, his face as

empty and innocent as a newborn babe's, "I think you'd actually be a terrific addition to our Youth Troop."

"Really?" I gawk at him, shocked, even though I imagined him saying those very words.

He touches my shoulder, and I flinch. I'm still not convinced this sick man isn't playing a trick on me. "I urge you to consider it. Come, look at them." He waves his hand across the window, and I can see the kids below. They're viciously beating a dummy with sticks, and stuffing erupts from its torso. I shudder. "Can't you see yourself among them?" He grins eerily. "*Guiding* them?"

"Well, I don't know, sir," I say, having a little fun. "I'm not convinced the Youth Troop is the best place for my specific talents."

"Please!" His bark makes me jump. The general is grasping frantically at my arms, shaking me, his voice verging on madness. And then he's shaking so hard I feel like my head might snap.

Refocus, Wisty! I remind myself. I suddenly realize that I might accidentally take this newfound power to places I hardly understand or can control.

"You need only name your price. I'll...I'll arrange for extra chocolate rations!" he yells, his eyes crazed with desperation.

I immediately start to salivate, remembering that divine, otherworldly chocolate from our days at the Brave New World Center, but then catch myself when I remember how freaking addicting the stuff was and how the N.O. used it for brain control. To extract all energy and euphoria from young minds.

It almost took me to the dark side.

"That won't be necessary, General. But I suppose I'll join anyway," I concede, wrenching myself from his grip as he nods, his mustache bobbing. "But only because you said *please*."

Chapter 45

Wisty

IF THERE'S ONE thing Youth Troops love, it's marching.

With my crisp white-and-red New Order uniform and my hair in two tight braids, I practice legs up, arms stiff, eyes dead, drill after drill after drill.

"Now," a horse-faced older boy barks after we've been at it for three hours, "we will review maneuvers to capture young Resisters." He goes down the line with a box, passing out equipment, but I can't make out what it is yet.

"Remember," he says, "the enemy will swerve, dodge, even beg. To eliminate this threat, place the wire against the neck and press the button."

I have no idea what he's talking about, but right then a door in one of the buildings opens up and dozens of puppies come bounding out of it, tongues waving in the air. I look around, and none of my Youth Troop peers even cracks a smile. They look like they're facing down a plague of locusts.

I'm uneasy about what all of this means—the N.O. has a history of using dogs as killer weapons—but I have a serious soft spot for all canines, and I can't help crouching down to pet one. The dog goes crazy, licking my hands and face, its little tail wagging a mile a minute.

And then, *zap!* The little dog collapses to the ground, seizing. *What the—?*

One of my N.O. comrades, a small pigtailed girl with missing front teeth, stands over him with some sort of stun-gun apparatus, grinning like a banshee, and then takes off for her next victim.

I look around and watch the other dogs yelping as the brainwashed kids gleefully stun them, and I feel the familiar heat building in my body, the anger reaching a boil. But now is *not* the time to flame out. I'm in the middle of a heavily guarded N.O. facility, and if I'm lucky, I just might get my chance to see The One. But trying not to let my rage get the best of me is literally making smoke come out of my ears.

Stop, Wisty. Slow down. Pause. I snap my fingers as if to break my swelling energy, to stop the eruption of flame, and suddenly—

Everyone stops moving. Everyone but me.

The puppies run around, barking happily again, but the sour-faced New Order Youth have all become statues with stun guns raised in midair, their faces petrified in expressions of evil glee.

Okay! Wasn't expecting that, *but it'll work.*

This is the perfect opportunity to take a look around the complex for The One. The last time I saw him, he boiled the ocean into a tsunami wave of terror—with Whit and me surfing on top of it—right before he vaporized my parents.

I sit, leaning against one of the unmoving kids as the stupidity of what I'm about to attempt really hits me. I'm not ready for this.

All I want to do is run from this place, and keep running until I'm free: run into my mother's arms, back into my childhood, to a place where the New Order never existed, and where I was never a witch, where I was never the one people were counting on.

But that's not how it is, and it's not how it's ever going to be again.

So I ignore every warning screaming through my body, every flight response my nerves are sending out in alert. Instead, I stand back up. Instead, I walk toward my fate, head held high. I am going to find the most powerful being in our universe, and, though it seems like suicide, I'm going to fight him.

Because I'm the only one who can.

I shoo the little dogs away and creep across the courtyard. I'm not sure if my immobilization spell affected everyone or just the trainees, and I'm not taking chances.

I inch my way to the edge of the building and stealthily peer around the corner.

And immediately pull back in fear and drop to a crouch.

Because there, across the grounds on his way into an imposing red building, I see *him*.

The One Who Is The One.

The clouds part in front of him, and his bald head gleams in the sunlight. He strides along confidently with a New Order comrade, and he *radiates* power—a ruthlessness that makes my resolve crack and shatter.

As they get closer, I can see him more vividly, his handsome face hard, his Technicolor eyes hypnotic.

My breath is virtually knocked out of me as I realize who's with him: none other than the weasel, Byron Swain. I look at the gravel rocks around my feet and consider lobbing one at his rodenty, traitorous little head.

That, or a lightning bolt.

Chapter 46

Whit

THE LOST ONES are preparing for dinner.

The valley is abuzz with activity as the zombie-eyed undead stroll back and forth to the forest, gathering bones for the fire.

Lost Children add brush; Lost Men, a tower of skulls. Do bones really burn? Apparently. An older Lost Woman gnashes her teeth at us and positions a long spear, sharpened at both ends, over the pile. A spit.

The only thing they have left to add is the meat.

Us.

Janine is with the Resistance kids on the other side of the fire pit, her hands wrapped tightly along a section of rope. A steady stream of tears is leaking out of her eyes, and she's no longer making a move to brush them away. The kids look shell-shocked and paralyzed, and I don't blame them.

How do you prepare to be eaten alive?

They've separated me from the others and bound me with twice the rope, so I can only assume I'll be the first to burn.

Feffer lies at my feet, her legs bound together and sticking straight up in the air. The dog howls, and the sound is full of despair; she had guessed at the Lost Ones' plans long before we did.

Shouts from the forest add to the din, and another chain of kids is dragged into the camp, a couple of them struggling hard against the ropes and passionately demanding justice. I sigh with relief to see that it's Sasha yelling, with Emmet on his heels. *They're alive—*

But not for long. My relief is immediately followed by an overwhelming queasiness. This is going to be the end of the *entire* Resistance.

"You're not really planning to eat us, are you?" I say to a passing Lost One, who looks around my age. Despite Celia's warnings, despite the feasting preparations, I can't really make myself believe it.

"Of course," the Lost One says, licking his scabby lips. "Why wouldn't we?"

"Because these are *people!*" I scream, near hysterics. "Because these people have emotions, and lives. You can't just go around *eating* them!"

"No?" he cocks his head, surveying the fire pit and the prey with the innocence of a child. Lost Ones obviously have no moral compass.

"I wish you were next," the Lost Girl with the low,

haunting voice says, tracing her decaying fingers along my arm. "You look *yummy*."

"You mean I'm *not* next?" I manage to get out.

"Of course not," she says matter-of-factly. "You're our savior. Why would we eat *you*?"

Chapter 47

Whit

"YOU ARE THE healer, aren't you, Whit?" The Lost Girl peers at me with her hollowed eyes, and I shiver as she touches my face, the flesh on her arm falling away from the bone. "Can you heal me? Fix all of us? Can you free us from the Shadowland?"

These poor creatures, I think, despite my revulsion. These decaying, monstrous beings somehow believe I can make them better.

But... what if I can? What if this is what I was brought here to do?

Something Mrs. Highsmith said echoes in my mind: *You shouldn't fear the dead.* Is this what she meant?

The girl reads my hesitation and pounces. "Help me, Whit. Set me free," she groans urgently.

The other Lost Ones, sensing that this girl might be awarded something they want, scramble over one another greedily. They plead to be the first to be saved, and paw at my face and still-bound arms. The stench closes in on me, and I'm gagging, trapped.

"I don't know how to help you!" I shout, panic rising in my voice.

A Lost Woman shoves the others aside, her stringy hair peeling back from her forehead, her yellow eyes haunted. She claws at my shoulders, shaking me. "If you are the child of the Prophecy, you must heal me!" she demands. "This wasn't part of the deal!"

"Don't listen to them, Whit!" Sasha shouts over the crowd, and I remember that he has a lot more experience with these creatures than I do. "Why do you think they're here? They don't deserve your mercy!"

"What do you mean, *this wasn't part of the deal?*" I turn back to the Lost Woman, still confused about how she and the others got this way.

"For strangling the children. I was supposed to live forever," she answers in a detached voice. "I want what I deserve."

"Children? You *murdered* them?" I whisper, thinking of Celia.

"I was only following The One's orders." She smiles, revealing blackened, chipped teeth with sharp points. "But I promise I won't do it again."

"And you think I'm just going to *heal* you, to send you back into the world?" I ask, bitterness creeping into my voice. The other Lost Ones eagerly shuffle toward me again at the mention of being healed.

"Don't you get it?" I shout. "This *is* what you deserve. It's not just your flesh that's rotting, it's your *souls*, because of what you've done. All of you. I wouldn't set you free even if you tortured me, if you ripped me apart limb from limb."

"We could arrange for that," the woman says darkly.

I steel myself for the attack, but it doesn't come. Instead, the Lost Ones lunge for the Resistance kids, wrenching Emmet and Sasha and the others to their feet.

Sasha pushes against them in fury, his hair whipping around his face, a revolutionary to the end. But Emmet, normally a big teddy bear, looks at me steely-eyed, his jaw set into tight resolve. He shakes his head once, as if to say, *No deals. Never give in. No matter what.*

"Whit!" Janine shouts as they seize her.

"Janine!" Her name tears through me.

She shakes her head. "It's okay. You'll survive this, and the Resistance will live on." She's trying to be so, so strong, but her arms grasp at the air in protest, and terror dances in her eyes. I can't pretend this'll end well.

The Lost Ones drag the group into an enclosed pen in front of me, untying their wrists from the rope. They actually *want* their prey to move around—something about tenderizing the meat—but the sharp metal mesh that lines the cage looks like it'll prevent any of them from breaking free.

The Lost Ones select the first kid—a boy around twelve with light, dirty hair—and drag him near the pit. He's struggling fiercely against these creatures, but they pin him down with ease, tying him to the roasting spit I saw earlier.

Panic erupts, and the kids in the pen get hysterical, throwing themselves against the cage, wailing to be freed, reaching out toward their friend on the stake, whose unthinkable fate awaits each and every one of us. But the Lost Ones only howl in response—a horrible, ear-shattering cacophony of pain that I can't shut out.

If I won't heal the Lost Ones, they'll force me to hear every shriek, to smell the sulfurous stench, to *feel* the whole grisly event as each of my friends goes up in flames. As the Resistance is entirely extinguished in a gruesome holocaust.

My body buzzes with grief, and my heart breaks in defeat.

"No!" I roar. I won't let this happen. I thrash against the ropes, and they gouge lines into my wrists. I summon all of my strength and buck frantically, but nothing budges. I'm in position to watch the horror show unfold.

My head hangs, despair washing over me, and just when the situation seems most dire, the Lost Girl who was talking to me earlier reappears, holding a bucket. And then, with a grisly smile plastered across her skeletal face, she slathers sauce and spices all over my dearest friends.

She's *basting* them.

Chapter 48

Whit

THE RED FOG presses in claustrophobically, and beyond, the bones of the forest stretch upward, like arms clawing their way out of this hell. Lost Ones swarm around us, and the smell of burnt hair gags me as they add discarded animal pelts to the flame. I ache for a spell, for a way out, but my magic doesn't seem to work on the dead. The fire pit grows hotter, and hope is just a pipe dream.

"Whit?" Janine whispers from the pen five feet in front of me, and I drag my eyes away from the macabre preparations and look down at her gorgeous, strangely calm face.

"Yeah?" I murmur.

"It's okay." She grips the metal mesh of the pen, her knuckles white with the effort. She needs to believe that it really is okay. But I can't. I can see the pit from here, and they're wrapping that poor boy tighter and tighter on the spit.

"What do you mean?" I ask, despair creeping into my voice. "Janine, look at where we are. *Nothing* is okay."

"It's going to be, though. Even if we don't make it," she says, that strong, determined look that I know so well returning to her eyes, "we'll still have won. Because we'll never be *this*." She looks around.

"You're right." I nod. "We'll never be like them."

"But before they . . . take us" — her voice cracks — "there's something I want to say." She takes a deep breath. "I think you're stupid. And crazy. And crazy stupid." I know she's desperately trying to find a way to make me smile, as if it's what she wants her last sight of me to be before a tragic end. "And I'll never forgive you for coming back here after you promised me a million years ago that you'd steer clear of this wretched place. What kind of pigheaded guy tries to take on not only the totally corrupt ruler of the Overworld but all of the evil in the Shadowland on top of it?" I chuckle weakly. It's what she wants me to do. "But I must be crazy stupid, too," she goes on, "because I actually think you can do it. Because you always made me believe in you in the worst of circumstances." She peers out at me through the cage, her face sincere.

The confession hangs between me and Janine as Sasha's hoarse voice screaming insults at the Lost Ones from the other side of the pen drowns out everything else.

"You're not stupid. Or crazy," I say. "You're amazing, and you —"

"And you're going to get out of here, you know," she interrupts. "And when you do, you'd better not give up the fight, because this is *not* the end, and —"

"We're *both* going to get out of here," I say stubbornly, even though it's clearly a lie. "And regardless of what happens, don't act like you're just some lackey falling by the wayside. You *are* this cause, Janine. You're the whole brains and passion behind it, and without you, The One would've wiped out every shred of the Resistance a long time ago." She looks at the ground, and I swallow. "And you're so, so beautiful," I say before I can stop myself, memorizing her features.

"Beautiful, yeah right." Janine manages a self-deprecating laugh, looking down at her body. "These grubby combat boots and this unwashed hair, and now the last image you have of me is with basting sauce."

"You look beautiful," I whisper, and mean it. She doesn't say anything, so I try for the lighter tone she'd been hoping to get out of me. "Who else can pull off apocalyptic chic?"

"Whit…" A tear slides down her cheek. "I think I love you," she whispers, her wide green eyes looking directly into mine. My heart lurches.

"Janine, I—"

But before I can say anything else, her eyes narrow, squinting at something behind me.

Oh no. Please don't let it be time yet.

Chapter 49

Whit

"WHAT?" I ASK. "Janine?" I look over my shoulder to see a Lost One approaching us through the red mist, a girl with a halo of wild dark curls, a girl who is kind of pretty, who, when she was alive, might even have been beautiful.

Or maybe she isn't a Lost One at all...?

Okay. I get it now. This is how it's going to go: this is the Angel of Death, come to carry us away from this grisly place, come to help us truly cross over. I guess it makes sense. Why did we ever think we'd make it out of the maze?

There's a bitter taste in my mouth as I feel all the fight finally go out of me. I was supposedly part of this epic Prophecy, but it was a lie. Just like everything else in this godforsaken world. I'm no different, no more special, than anyone else.

With anguish I think of my family. How will Wisty know? Will she think I've abandoned her? And what will my parents do, now that I've failed them?

If I was meant to die, if the Prophecy was all a hoax, I wish I could've just gone out with my parents when they were executed. Like a hero. Like a man. Instead of as a withering part of a miserable, barbaric, *pathetic* act of bestiality.

I shut my eyes, and the angel whispers my name. I wince. The truth is, I'm still not ready. No, I'm not ready for this at all.

But the voice is sweet, soothing. It sounds familiar, actually, like it's something I've been waiting for all my life. Realization hits me like a sledgehammer to the chest.

I am a total freaking idiot. *Of course she came.*

"Celia!" I shout. I see the hurt wash over Janine's face, and I cringe.

After my outburst, I shoot an anxious glance at the Lost Ones, but they seem too preoccupied to have noticed Celia or the disruption.

That, or maybe she really isn't here and I'm just hallucinating.

Emmet is on a pole farther down the line from me and Janine, and I see his eyes widen at the sight of this shimmering apparition. So I haven't totally lost it yet, at least.

Celia looks paler than before, and flickery. More like a ghost than an angel, to be honest.

"You're not . . . *Lost* now, are you?" I whisper.

She draws back from me, a look of disgust on her face. "Not a chance, Whit. I'm not a murderer; I was murdered."

I sigh with relief and then realize this could be our

ticket out. "I'm so glad you're here. We don't have much time, and—"

"Neither do I, Whit," she cuts in. "I'm sorry, but I can't bail you out this time. My light is already fading."

I glance at a Lost One, the empty sockets of its eyes gaping and emotionless. It licks the raw flesh where its lips should be, and panic builds in my chest. She wouldn't just leave us, would she?

Celia strokes my cheek, her touch lighter than air. I wish I could feel it. Then her hand falls away abruptly. "I'm sure you'll be fine, Whit." She glances at Janine. "You and your girlfriend." Her voice is detached, devoid of its usual sweetness, and her words slice through my heart.

"Celia, wait!"

Then the light goes out completely and Celia is gone again, and all of my hope with her.

Chapter 50

Wisty

TOOTHBRUSH IN HAND, I'm with my fellow New Order Youths, scrubbing the barracks inch by inch. Even though they're already spotless. Even though we scrubbed them for four hours yesterday and the day before.

My comrades, in their crisp uniforms and ribboned hair, are way more social than I would've thought. Contrary to the ideals of the New Order, during barracks detail they're positively chatty. Many of the girls have especially warmed up to me now that I'm one of them, a sort of older sister even, and I'm starting to learn that inside each programmed killing machine of the New Order Youth is a scared, manipulated child, brainwashed into submission.

Kathy's going on about the flirty comment Joseph made to Naomi after drills yesterday, and we're all kind of giggling when, without warning, the door to the barracks bangs open on its metal hinges, the hard wood slamming loudly against the wall.

There is an almost audible collective intake of breath as Pearce stalks in, his white-blond hair combed slickly off his forehead, his expression impossibly sinister.

"Well!" Pearce trumpets, clapping his hands together loudly like an enthusiastic camp counselor. The girl next to me flinches at the sound. "It's everyone's favorite day! Evaluation day! How's the cleaning coming, gang?" His smile is manic as he peeks into corners and behind bed-posts, scanning for offending dirt.

One of the younger kids whimpers, but everyone else is silent, eyes trained forward, shoulders hunched into themselves... anything to melt into the background.

I tense up, white noise flooding my ears and goose bumps erupting on my arms. I keep my head down and wait to be exposed. Someone finally gave me up.

But this doesn't seem to be about me after all. Pearce takes his time surveying the quarters, then squats down by one of the boys, surveying his work.

"You missed a spot," he points out with a smile, and the boy seems to shake all over. He furiously polishes the offending area with his toothbrush, but I can see there's a yellow wet spot forming on the seat of his crisp white uniform.

"There, there," Pearce coos. "No need for theatrics. This is what's called making an example. Very honorable thing you're doing, you realize."

The boy knows what's next. We all know. The kid's lip quivers as he threatens to dissolve into sobs. And as Pearce leans toward the boy, I picture the way the giant's face peeled back from his skull, and—

"Don't!" I gasp, scrambling to my feet. Kathy shakes her head at me in warning, alarm in her eyes, but I can't stop. "Just leave him alone. Please—"

Pearce whips around to face me, sparing the kid. Anger dashes across his face, but it's quickly replaced by delight— a spider that's found a fly tangled in its web.

A ravenous spider.

"What have we here?" Pearce purrs in my direction. "A new recruit?" His cold eyes hold me captive, challenging me, and I'm struck once again by how attractive he'd be if he didn't radiate evil in that bright smile.

I look down at the floor as he strides across the dimly lit barracks. My cheeks heat up under my blond-haired disguise. Does he know it's me? It's the longest I've ever kept a glamour going, but I'm still afraid there's some of Wisty showing through.

He circles me like a hawk homing in on its prey and stops behind me. I brace myself for the strike, teeth chattering.

Instead I nearly jump when I feel his hands on my shoulders, moving over my throat threateningly, drifting down my arms. Nothing has ever felt so unnatural, so *wrong*.

"We have certain policies new recruits have to follow around here, certain...initiations," he says, almost bored.

My whole body trembles with fear and adrenaline and hatred at his touch.

I could annihilate you, I think. *I could throw a ball of fire, burn you down to cinder if you don't get your slimy paws off me.*

But he doesn't, and I don't. Because I can't blow my cover. Because I can't waste my M just yet, and because — though I don't want to be — I'm scared, really scared, of this monster.

So his hands sit there on my arms, declaring their silent victory, and my skin crawls.

"It must be a challenge to adapt to life in the barracks, mmm?" he whispers quietly, almost tenderly. "I can imagine how hard it must be when everyone is watching you all of the time, cataloging your every move." His fingers trace circles around my freckles, and I flinch. "The One is adamant that I report any and all troublemakers immediately. It's very important to him that we maintain order. But you're not going to be any trouble, are you?" he whispers harshly into my ear, and I feel bile rising.

I turn to face him and look him in the eye. "You disgust me," I spit, and my voice doesn't falter.

His ice-blue snake's eyes flash. "*I* disgust *you,* pet? Which one of us is scrubbing floors?"

Then he lurches forward, mouth twisted into a sneer, and . . . he kisses me.

No — that's too polite for what he does. Pearce plants his lips on mine, gripping the back of my head fiercely, and shoves his tongue into my mouth. It's the vilest thing I've ever experienced.

Pearce sneers, drawing back with a repulsive smirk on his face. "Wasn't that sort of...*hot?*" I am speechless with revulsion and shock. "No, I don't think you're going to be any trouble at all." He smiles with satisfaction.

I want to wash my mouth out with lye. Or, better yet, turn him into a sponge. A grimy, dirty, bacteria-ridden one. Still, I remember all the power it took out of my brother just to keep Pearce's magic at bay, and I don't have that kind of energy to waste.

Instead I spit on the floor and go back to scrubbing the tile with my toothbrush while the other kids look on, mouths agape. Pearce marches out, his shiny black boots scuffing up my nice clean floor.

Right now I've got someone bigger to worry about, but you'll get yours, too, Pearce.

I promise.

Chapter 51

Wisty

I'M FEELING UTTERLY violated, and I can't stop tasting Pearce's gross, papery lips, but I try to put it out of my head as I sneak across the courtyard. There's no more time to waste. I have to get to The One, and soon, before Pearce becomes a bigger problem than he already is.

I need help. And unfortunately that means I need Byron Annoy-Your-Face-Off Swain, a kid I don't exactly want to be indebted to, since the guy could squeeze water from a rock if it meant something was in it for him.

After Byron finishes his daily drills, I tail him to the stock building behind the barracks, careful that no one's watching. I wish I could find a more secretive location, but I think this is the best we're going to do in a place that's crawling with armed guards. It could also be the only time I get him alone.

As I slink through the door, Byron's leaning against a shelf, awkwardly trying to feign nonchalance. He looks as officious as ever, with his crisp New Order uniform and his smarmy expression. Was he...expecting me?

"Wisty." He nods at me, not giving anything away, and I find myself once again questioning Byron's true motives. I knew he recognized me when they brought me in, but he hasn't even tried to connect with me since then. And here he is, looking completely *un*surprised that I'm sneaking around after him in a place where we could both be killed.

I look behind me. Maybe Byron has his own spies. "You wish to speak with me?" he presses.

Byron never changes, does he? I tried to train him to talk like a normal person when he was a Resistance member, but apparently my efforts were completely in vain.

Since he started out as a New Order spy, I'm still never sure who Byron's really working for—but I'll take my chances this time. If he doesn't cooperate, I could always test out a little more mind control, but since he's spent what seems like forever making passes at me, I'm guessing this one's in the bag.

"Hey, B., what's up?" I say as casually as possible. "Here's the deal. Now that you're back on the inside, I need you to get me on palace detail. I'm too out of shape to be running those drills, and I'd honestly rather be scrubbing toilets than hurting puppies." It's probably best not to lay out all my real motive cards, just in case Swain's seriously back on team N.O. "So you'll pull some strings—cool?" I've found that Byron responds best when I don't leave much room for discussion.

"I'm aware that your little drill routine is probably wearing thin. You want to get up close and personal with The One Who Is The One and the elite regimen, do you not? And you honestly think that you'll survive this?"

I shift uncomfortably. Am I that much of an open book? "Will you get me in or what?"

He gives me a long, serious look, then snickers. I'm right back to wanting to sock him, per usual. "Is it possible Her Highness, The Chosen One, is once again asking help from lowly little me?" He smirks. "Imagine my great surprise. Maybe you want to say *please*, Wisty, and remember all the favors I've done for you in the past."

I bite my tongue, studying him. A single exposed lightbulb swings from the ceiling, and the sense of being in an interrogation room isn't lost on me. He could have the place bugged. Who knows who he's working for? This could be a trap—

Deep breath. You have to trust *someone*, Wisty. This could be your last chance.

"Look, Byron," I say calmly, rationally, "I know we haven't always been on the best of terms, but this is serious. This is the big time. Everything before this was just training leading up to this moment. I'm going to get him this time. I'm going to take on the greediest, most corrupt tyrant the world's ever known." I put a hand on Byron's and summon my revolutionary voice. "Don't you want to be part of that?"

He perches on the table in the corner and crosses his

arms, unmoved. He purses his lips as if waiting for a better offer. My patience? Out the window.

Time for a different approach.

"Would you like to be a rodent, Swain?" I ask. "Because it's been a long time since I turned you back from a weasel, and frankly I think the look really worked for you, really meshed with your personality type."

Byron takes out some new techie gadget and waves it threateningly. "And would *you* like *me* to call in the New Order officials right now and have you thrown back behind bars? It would just take the touch of a button. You forget that I'm the one who has power here, Wisty. That it's *you* asking *me* for help."

I roll my eyes. "Are we still playing that game? *Hello*— I'm trying to get *closer* to The One. The One, who was going to fry you up as soon as he was done with you. And you're going to...what? Just swing back to the traitorous side and send in the troops?"

Byron shrugs, vague as ever. "A man's gotta do what a man's gotta do."

Something's off, even for smarmy Byron. "Why are you being so weird?" I demand. "You seemed almost, well, *normal* last time I saw you, and now you're back to this passive-aggressive charade. What's going on? Are you okay?"

Byron shrugs, silent. Something is seriously up if the weasel doesn't have a grating comeback.

"Byron?"

"You're acting as if you care about my well-being," he whines.

I sigh. It's so easy to forget that the weasel has human emotions. "I'm sorry. It's just that there's not a lot of time. Forgive me if I'm not coming off as warm and fuzzy as I usually do." I roll my eyes to emphasize the irony.

Silence.

"Come on, B. You and I have been through hell and back together. You know I care."

A cloud passes over his face. "I heard about your little lip-locking session with Pearce," Byron mumbles.

"You mean when that snake *assaulted* me?" I'm incredulous. "Yeah, Swain, I'm really drooling over that baby killer and his creepy cold hands. He *attacked* me, but I see that that part of the gossip didn't make it through to you." Byron doesn't answer, which just makes me fume. "Why do you care anyway?" I challenge.

"I guess I just thought we had something, Wisty," he says quietly, his pride clearly wounded.

Oh. *That.* "We're talking about *life and death* here, Byron, and you're telling me you're *jealous?*"

Byron's face immediately shuts down, and he strides over to the shelves, grabbing armfuls of stun devices, ropes, and a megaphone for the next round of drills.

I keep my distance on the other side of the small room, watching his agitated, jerky movements with guilt. I don't want to hurt Byron, but I don't want to like him either. That intense connection we had playing onstage together at the Stockwood Music Festival frankly still freaks me out.

"Byron, don't take it personally, I just—"

"Whatever," he says, back to his clipped New Order demeanor. He turns to go.

"Hey," I call after him, "just get me in the palace, okay?"

"I'll see what I can do," he says noncommittally. Then he turns back around. "And, Wisty...?" Byron's face looks suddenly grave, and dread settles in the pit of my stomach.

"What?" My voice sounds high and thin.

He chews his lip as if deciding something, and I almost shake him. "You need to work fast. My intel says Whit's in serious trouble in the Shadowland. You don't have much time to deal with The One if you want to save him."

Chapter 52

Whit

TORCHES BOB, BLURRY in my peripheral vision. A bonfire belches into the bloodred twilight. Fire is all around us, licking at our skin and lighting our expressions of terror, and the stench of the gathering Lost Ones, of their rotting flesh and dark intentions, is truly unbearable.

The shrill intensity of their chants builds in tune with my racing heart.

My arms ache from the weight of my body, and I flinch away from the hands of death that reach for me. I'm strung up high on some massive wheel, an ancient torture device that keeps my arms and legs spread wide, my body exposed, so that these putrid creatures can spin me around, touch me, and be healed.

Below me, the stage is set for an ominous Holiday Feast, and the Resistance kids are bound on their circle of spits. Sasha shouts fight anthems mixed with obscenities at the Lost Ones in a never-ending babble of protest, and Emmet looks heartbreakingly sad but determined not to make a scene. If the Resistance is going down, it's going down with honor, if he has anything to say about it. Most of the other kids are sobbing uncontrollably, but Janine is resigned, her strong face a mask.

She won't meet my eyes.

Hands cover me, and the ancient wheel turns, spinning me left, then right, so I have to strain my neck to see anything. My heart longs to fight, to keep fighting until my last breath, but I'm so weak and dizzy and there are so many of them, rabid with need.

How can this be the end of everything? Some child of the Prophecy I've turned out to be.

The Lost Ones stamp the ground, growing impatient. The awful chanting reaches a fever pitch, the ravenous howls slicing into the evening, but the youngest child's screams drown out all else as they drag him toward the pit to be roasted alive.

We're done for.

Chapter 53

Wisty

WELL, I HAVE to hand it to Byron: I asked, and he delivered. I got exactly what I wanted—a cleaning position in the elite apartments of the palace compound. But somehow I'm not quite as happy scrubbing toilets as I thought I'd be.

The compound is a solid brick building, part fortress, part palace, and it takes me two days of entering through the heavily guarded gates, passing under the metal detectors, and waiting in the steel-sealed holding cell before a fellow worker loans me a key to go through the side entrance that leads straight to the elite complex.

The high-ceilinged, echoing corridors are exactly what you'd expect from the New Order, with clean linoleum floors and ultra-sanitary surfaces. The private apartments, on the other hand, are an entirely different story.

The upper echelons of our society may be a buttoned-up bunch, but they're not always the most hygienic in their personal quarters—take it from one who knows. *Be careful what you* influence *for, I guess.*

But it all pays off in the end, because after scouring, sanitizing, and polishing my fifteenth toilet, I'm assigned the proverbial pot o' gold: *his* personal lavatory.

I stand in the doorway for at least ten minutes, listening. This is my chance to find some weakness, some vulnerability, to riffle through The One's most private, hidden items, but at first I can't even move for fear of being caught.

The One's apartment is shockingly spare, almost sterile. There's hardly any furniture, and what's here is a simple, sturdy black. The claustrophobic red paint vibrating on the wall is as crimson as a crime scene or an open wound. The only things of note are the mirrors: gold-framed, one on each wall. They're presumably so His Baldness will always have a place to gaze adoringly at himself, but somehow they give a person the feeling that he's looking *out* of them, watching, instead of looking in.

A narrow bed is the only item in the windowless bedroom. I reach out to it tentatively, as if it's a sleeping monster, ready to snap off my hand. Though it looks hard, it's surprisingly soft, giving under my touch. Are the sheets warm, or is it my imagination? It's impossible to imagine him sleeping here. Or sleeping at all.

The floor creaks below my feet, and my heart leaps out of my chest. I strain to listen for a hint of voices approaching, but all I can hear is the blood surging in my ears. I search the corners for hidden cameras and expect to trip a booby trap with every movement. I've never been so jumpy in my life.

I know I have to buck up, get it together, do what I came here to do, but all I keep thinking is, The One tortures kids for minor infractions and curses thousands of people with bleeding, open sores. What kind of horrors await a staff member caught snooping in his most personal items?

In the bathroom mirror (gold-framed, enormous), a lost-looking, frightened girl stares back at me, threatening to bolt, but I see my parents' faces there, too, pleading and hopeful. I splash my face in the ice-cold water of the stainless-steel sink, swallow my fear, and carefully open a cupboard.

It's strange, you don't think of evil people having personal things, and it's impossible to imagine what The One might have stored in these bathroom drawers, what ghastly souvenirs from a lifetime of cruelty. But the items I do find — including dentures and Technicolor contact lenses — are bizarrely mundane and almost funny in the way they suggest self-consciousness.

I'm pawing through these ordinary articles, fascinated, when a floorboard creaks in the hallway. I don't dare breathe as the footsteps get louder, louder, almost upon me ... and then echo down the hall toward the other apartments. I sigh, turning back to my task.

Peering into the cupboard again, I notice a tiny box that I somehow missed before, and inside it, a silver key. It seems impossible that I could locate what door or safe this small key unlocks, but I remember a desk by the entryway, and when I walk across the apartment and slide the key into the hole in the drawer, it turns with a satisfying *click*.

When they say "too easy," this is what they mean.

Inside there's an odd collection of mementos, none of them mind-blowing, but apparently important to The One nonetheless. They're special. Personal. *Human,* as hard to believe as it seems.

There's an award for extraordinary abilities in a science contest, a picture of a young and smiling One with a small girl (possibly his sister?), and a certificate of artistic appreciation recognizing young talent. Buried farther down, I also find a report of difficulties in social development, a handwritten note from a teacher about "disturbing demonstrations" that frightened other students, and a letter of expulsion.

I want to keep digging, want to find more about the boy who would grow up to be the greediest, most powerful being in the Overworld, but time is running out and I haven't even cleaned anything yet.

I carefully replace all of the documents, but as I start to close the drawer, I glimpse the yellowed edge of a photograph caught in the side. I bite my lip, checking my watch. It's a risk, but one last look couldn't hurt.

It takes me several minutes to work the picture out of the crack it's jammed in, and when I do, I draw a sharp intake of breath. I lean against the desk, mesmerized.

It appears to be another family photograph. This one is

taken from farther away, when The One was a bit older but still a boy. There's an older man in the picture, with jutting cheekbones and an upright posture. The man is smiling— wide but strangely lacking emotion, as if the grin is taped on.

The man's hand is on the boy's shoulder, near his neck, gripping at the kid's clothing and pressing him forward for the pose. Gripping hard.

The boy in the picture—The One, which is still weird to think about—is not smiling. At all. His eyes are different than in the earlier photo with the young girl, too. They understand more. Those eyes have seen terrible things.

And here's the part that's most chilling: the older man's eyes and nose have been scratched out with a black pen, so that a skeleton seems to peer back at me, its grotesque grin hiding all of its secrets.

Hands shaking, I shove the photo back into the crack and then hastily scrub the already sparkling toilet. I slink out of the apartment, my mind whirring with the knowledge that The One was once a kid, once had friends and family, once smiled and ached and *felt* things, rejection among them.

And once had a father whose smile was not a smile at all.

I'm so caught up in my thoughts that I don't even see His Coldness coming down the hallway until I nearly walk smack into him.

Chapter 54

Wisty

THE CARPET IN the elite complex corridor is bloodred, with a swirling, repeating *O* pattern that is making me dizzy and nauseous. My work shoes, once bleach-white and spotless, are grimy and disgusting. I stand slightly pigeon-toed, a fact that's never annoyed me until now.

I know I probably shouldn't be so preoccupied with the minute details of my feet. I came here to deal with Him, to use my power, to rid the world of this evil, but the truth is, I'm utterly petrified to look up at The One.

Has the air around him always been so freezing? Has he always seemed so tall and menacing? Does he always wear those dark suits, so perfectly pressed? Could he always suck the air right out of my lungs?

He's so *cold,* so evil, and he waits me out silently, his tall figure unmoving. I think it'll go on like this forever, until he finally breaks the spell with his calm, patronizing voice.

"Don't be afraid, child. You should be proud of yourself for achieving such an important post at a young age. Many New Order Youth will never experience the great honor of entering my private quarters, let alone tending my toilet."

I can't believe what I'm hearing. Achieving an important post? Cleaning toilets? Nothing about destroying me, or using my Gift, or being an utter disappointment?

Before I can squeak out a response, The One turns on his heel and strides away, carefree, whistling the N.O.'s national anthem as he enters his apartment.

I let out a long, uneasy sigh. I hadn't realized I'd been holding my breath.

Should I feel relieved that he didn't recognize me, or…

Am I really that forgettable?

Chapter 55

Wisty

I SLAM AROUND the barracks, furious with myself. I'm a tightly stretched rubber band of built-up energy, ready to snap.

I pace the linoleum floor, berating myself for being the girl that every lame teacher—including The One—pegged me to be: a dropout. If there's one thing in my life I needed to finish, it was this. I had him, right in front of me, right where I wanted him—my chance! And what did I do?

I studied my feet.

Some child of the Prophecy I've turned out to be. I'm on the verge of catching fire, I can feel it, and to release the anger I whip around, kick one of the solid-wood bunks, and crumple onto the floor, swallowing a scream of pain.

This just keeps getting better, doesn't it?

I roll onto my side, wincing, and take slow, calming breaths. The One's face appears before me, and fear falls away from me like water. I see through his mask, see through to the dentures and the color contacts, see that it is just a human face, aging and powerless to stop time. A tiny, insignificant blot on humanity who will wither and die without *my* power, *my* M—something I'll never give up.

I put my hands on the sides of his face, almost tenderly, and terror flickers in his eyes. He sees the change in me, the control. A flash of energy illuminates the whole room.

I laser in on his thoughts, but I don't even need to waste energy warping them. He knows I've won, that there is no greater sorceress in existence; that to live, he must fix his misdeeds.

His head falls into his hands, shame overwhelming him. He even cries. *Can we ever forgive him?* he asks. All he needed was a bit of coaxing, and now things can go back to the way they were before....

A sob cuts through the fantasy, and I blink away the image of the defeated One. Another cry pierces the air—that hopeless, scared shriek of a child who's lost all hope. I scramble to my feet, wincing for my wounded toe, and peer outside the barred windows of the barracks at the commotion in the courtyard below. My view is slightly obscured by a watchtower, but I can still see him.

Pearce. I grip the bars with white knuckles, seething with white-hot rage.

The nauseating serpent towers over a small boy and holds a book by its spine in disgust. The kid looks at the ground, obviously expecting the worst, and the rest of the children are gathered, wide-eyed and frozen, much like they were when he entered the barracks the other day.

Pity tugs at my heart. Can I honestly blame these N.O. Youth for their evil acts, for following The One's orders when the environment of terror obviously keeps them so rigidly in check?

"What have we here?" Pearce says, his words clipped and cheerful but loud enough for the whole compound to hear. "*New Order, 1, 2, 3: The Soldier's Path.* Interesting choice of reading material. It's a pity that all reading material for level-one recruits is strictly *banned*," he says, a threat creeping into his voice.

"B-b-but, it's for *you!*" the kid stutters in protest. "For you and The One! I was just studying. I just . . . I just want to be the most exemplary New Order Youth I can be, sir!"

Pearce scoffs, pacing out of my view. "Literacy rots the brain, I'm afraid. And a rotten mind is of no use to the New Order. Sadly, there must be consequences. We'll have to demonstrate to these other rule-abiding youths the detriments of disobedience."

I crane my neck through the bars, just in time to see Pearce step forward and grab the boy by his temples.

"No!" I yell, fire shooting through my fingertips, but only enough to melt the bars.

Pearce looks around sharply, but it's too late. The kid's eyes roll backward, and in less than a second his face is only ash. The rest of the Youth Troop gasps. Clearly these are new recruits who haven't witnessed this rampant cruelty up close before.

I bet none of them will forget the lesson.

Neither will I. A kid. He was just a kid.

I step back from the fire-damaged window, numb. My stomach twists with the fresh realization of what The One and his despicable henchman are capable of. It's a crushing contrast to my daydream, but it rallies my conviction at the same time.

I have to deal with The One, because crimes like this, murders like this, go on day after day in this cowardly new world, and if what they say is true, if I'm The One With The Gift, The One Who Can Stop The One, who am I to go on pretending it'll get better? When kids are dying, what right do I have to be afraid?

This time, *I'm going out to get him.*

Chapter 56

Wisty

I WAKE WITH a start, a sense of urgency making my mind hum.

I forgot to return the keys to the palace after cleaning the elite apartments this afternoon.

And no one noticed.

Around me in the barracks, my fellow N.O. comrades snooze in their bunks, looking impossibly innocent. It's very late — around two or three a.m. — and I should probably lie back down and dream of another toilet-filled day ahead of me, should probably get some rest before the morning punishment comes, when they realize I still have the keys.

But I'm far too restless for that. My fingertips tingle — I can feel my M *growing.* An exhilarating energy is coursing through me, and I have to act on it. I'm finally ready to confront The One, and there's no better time than Right. This. Minute.

I dress in the dark and tiptoe past the slumbering kid soldiers, sneaking out of the barracks and into the starless night. I slink along the brick buildings, pausing as still as a statue and pressing into the wall as the searchlight passes over me.

There is a group of N.O. guards making noise in the courtyard, their good spirits and stumbles suggesting alcohol and banned activity. One shoves another as I watch from the shadows, and the soldiers screech with laughter. If I'm caught on forbidden grounds it's punishable by expulsion, and catching guards breaking rules would probably mean something a whole lot worse for me.

I could kill them, I think, shocking myself with this realization that I would do *anything* to get to The One right now. More than that—I have the power to.

But they're already distracted, and I've reached the side gate. There's no room for fear as I quietly take the palace keys from my belt loop and unlock the door, adrenaline and the daydream of defeating The One urging me forward.

I pad up the stairs to the imperial suite, rehearsing over and over in my head what I'll say, how I will open the door silently and stealthily, how I won't hesitate to zap The One with a brain bolt so powerful he'll drop dead on contact.

Instead I'm totally unprepared when I reach The One's door to find him, the picture of cool nonchalance, leaning against his doorway.

Expecting me.

He takes a small ceremonial bow, an amused smile

playing across his lips, and says, "I really am proud of you and how well you do toilets, Wisteria Allgood. It's a step in the right direction anyway. So is that New Order uniform. It looks stunning on you. Truly."

"But—," I falter. "You mean . . . you knew it was me?"

The One sneers and manages to look both furious and amused at once. "Of course I knew it was you. I didn't want to push you if you weren't ready to join me quite yet."

He studies his creepily long, manicured nails absently. "I wasn't willing to wait much longer, and I'm delighted you sought me out at last. So are you now? Ready to join me, Wisteria?"

Chapter 57

Whit

MY EYES ARE shut tight against the grisly horrors about to take place, but when the Lost Ones' fierce chanting stops suddenly, I force them open.

Sasha and Emmet are gaping at something in the distance, and I follow their gaze with a mix of hope and fear.

What I see takes my breath away.

An extraordinary light grows on the horizon, breaking through the bleak fog. I squint against the bright radiance, and it's Celia in all her glory, racing toward us from over the hills with an army of Half-lights in her wake.

There is a long, silent moment when the Lost Ones freeze in place, their faces distorted with distress. Not a soul moves as the light pulses onward.

And then all hell breaks loose.

The Lost Ones stumble forward, dazed, pulled toward this age-old enemy as moths to flame. The Half-lights surge to meet them, and the forces of light and dark collide in one blinding, writhing mass. An explosion of energy bursts forth like a sun reemerging after an eclipse, too painful to look at directly.

It's over in an instant.

Then the Lost Ones tear off, frantic and screeching, and beat a path of destruction through the bone forest. Defeated.

The Half-lights take the camp and get to work untying the kids from the stakes and putting out the raging fires. Sasha is already singing songs of victory and gathering together the saved Resistance, but I can see that his cheeks are wet with tears.

And Celia, my Celia, races to my side, her deft fingers flitting over my body though I can't quite feel them, undoing the straps and releasing the levers. She's still a Half-light, not quite solid, but in the Shadowland, it seems, her touch has more weight; she can move these objects constructed by other creatures of the Underworld.

"Celes, how did you...? Why did they...?"

I'm babbling with relief, unable to get a coherent word out.

"The balance had shifted," she murmurs, still working, her mouth twisting in concentration. She looks up at me. "In the Shadowland, what's good becomes more pure over time and what's bad just rots with its evil."

"So you're at your strongest when they're at their weakest?"

Celia nods. "When we're all together like this"—she gestures at the Half-lights—"the light wins."

Soon I'm standing face-to-face with her, and I feel...
whole again. And I've finally put something together. "It
was you before, wasn't it? When our parents were executed
and Wisty and I were supposed to go down with them.
There was that blinding, painful light, and The One was
on his knees, screaming. Wisty and I fell. Like falling into
death, only light caught us. It was you. You and the other
Half-lights."

"Sort of. It was a little more complicated than that,
but...it doesn't matter now." She puts her hand on my lips
and smiles that gorgeous, sweet smile that lights up her
whole face. "I mean, aren't you going to say it's good to
see me?"

I look into her teasing eyes, put my hands around her face.
"Celia, it *is* so, so good to see you." I'm melting into her eyes.

"I'm sorry I had to abandon you earlier, Whit—"

"Forget it. I know there's a reason for everything in this
insane world, even if I don't understand it. All that matters
is that I'm—I'm *feeling* you again."

Sasha comes up behind me and yells, "Awwww!" in his
sappiest, most obnoxious voice. He jabs me in the ribs.
Emmet joins us, looking embarrassed, but wiggles his eyebrows approvingly anyway.

Janine appears behind them, smiling, but not with her
eyes.

I look around at the camp—the bonfire remnants and
animal bones and menacing forest beyond. The scene still
appears eerie in the red mist of the Underworld sky, but

the glow from all of the Half-lights moving around and making sure the kids are all right makes everything seem almost . . . safe. Like finding out the monster in the room is just your imagination when you switch on the light.

Almost like we're not in the land of the dead.

Chapter 58

Whit

UNDER THE PRETENSE of scouting out a trail, Celia and I walk hand in hand away from the group. With her next to me now, I can almost forget about finding my parents, about Wisty risking her life to take down The One, about nearly being roasted alive, about Janine. I can convince myself that there's just us, two carefree teenagers in love, walking into the wilderness.

We stop at the edge of the forest, and Celia peers up at me, her eyes swimming. There's so much I have to tell her, but she's looking at me like she already knows everything I'm feeling, everything I've been through, so for now I just want to savor this moment.

Celia lifts her chin up and I inhale her scent, dizzy with love and need. I put my lips against hers so tenderly, but I can't feel her at all; she's only air. And then Celia leans into me and we do something I've been thinking about,

211

dreaming about, since the last time I saw her—we *merge* into one soul, one being.

And it takes my breath away. I've never felt so close to anyone, so *whole,* and it's as if my heart is expanding and being crushed at once.

I feel *her.*

Everywhere.

Chapter 59

Whit

I WANT TO stay like this forever, enveloped in Celia's warmth and safe in her cocoon of light, but it's only a few seconds before I feel her slipping away from me again, our cells realigning in our separate bodies.

"Oh man, that's...just...incredible," I breathe into Celia's wild hair as we finally break apart.

"Best thing ever," she agrees. "The living are really missing out." She laughs but then catches herself; it's less funny when she remembers which side of the divide I'm on. "Do you think maybe..." Her eyes search mine, uncertain. "Don't you think it might be time to move on?"

"Where are we moving on *to*?" I ask, trying to keep the hurt out of my voice. "Celia, you can't leave here, right? I don't want to go back again without you. I want to be with you...forever."

As I say it, I notice Janine, watching us walking back, her jaw set and eyes clear with understanding.

Celia tenses and intertwines her fingers with mine. She doesn't say anything for a moment, and I know she's considering the possibilities. I squeeze her hand as best I can, but then she breaks away and turns on me. "Don't you think I want that, too? It's not something I can just *decide*, Whit. You can't survive here!"

"But you can destroy the Lost Ones, right?" I plead. "We can live here safely. Together."

Celia shakes her head. "That's not how it works, baby. Without their darkness, the Shadowland is out of balance. The good doesn't come without the bad... all of it passes through here. Without them, the passages between worlds begin to close. They're already closing."

"Celes, you're not making any sense, I swear—"

"Think of it like this, Whit: we need them to continue to exist so that our light doesn't go out completely."

My breath catches. "It'll never go out, Celia," I choke. "I couldn't bear it."

She smiles, but it's a sad smile filled with longing and untold secrets.

"We'll deal with that when the time comes," she whispers. "But right now, there are things you need to see in the Shadowland. Things all of you need to see," she says as we approach the group of Resistance kids. "The others can come too. You too, Janine," she adds as an afterthought.

Janine nods and looks away, and my ears heat up in shame. I want to take her hand, to explain, but I can't.

Chapter 60

Wisty

I WALK TOWARD him, head held high, and for a moment time stops as The One and I take in each other, the disheveled, determined girl and the demonic dictator towering over her.

The fluorescent light flickers, casting gray-green shadows on his face. He looks garish, possessed.

Evil.

My confidence is zapped by his cold, cruel stare. *I can't do this.* I step back from him, muscles twitching like a deer ready to bolt.

I turn, but The One grabs my wrist, lightning quick, nearly snapping the bones.

"Time's up, child. I'm giving you the *choice,* the *opportunity* of an apprenticeship." He twists my arm, his grasp fierce and unsparing. "Say you'll take it, Wisteria. I'm losing—"

"Ah!" I grimace in pain.

"—patience."

I swallow hard, concentrating all of my focus on the fantasy, the one where I'm able to strip The One completely of his power. It felt so real, so attainable, earlier. I have The Gift, right? I'm The Chosen One.

So why do I feel so small? Why do I feel myself shrinking from him, ready to forfeit?

And then in a flash I see that kid's skin peel back from his head. I look at the cold glee on The One's angular face, drunk with power, and I realize that there's no time to hesitate, that it has to happen *now*.

The fire is building within me, ready to spark, and I laser in on him just like in the daydream. I distill every ounce of M I've been saving up, and I release it on this pathetic tyrant.

The One's eyes widen as he looks down at my arm, flames licking through his grip. The heat is there, the fire, but it's *more* than that. It's *control*.

He makes a choking sound, and I feel the raw electric power pulse from my fingertips and connect with him. The One flies backward, crashing against the wall. He hovers several feet off the ground, clenching his manicured fingers and writhing in real pain.

It's awful to watch, and I want to stop, to back off — I'm not connecting with his thoughts, can't remember how — but I can't look away. This is what I came here to do.

I send one final surge, and his limbs convulse as if zapped by a bolt of lightning, and he collapses in a heap on the hallway floor.

I'm too scared to move, too spent by this power to see what I've done. I don't know what I'm capable of.

Could he be…dead?

But as soon as the thought crosses my mind, The One springs back up, his eyes insanely bright, and laughs weakly, the skin stretched tight across his stiff jaw, a puppet of horror.

"You're doing it all wrong, Wisty. Backward. Oh, how it *pains* me."

Then, as if he's decided to relieve me of a great burden: "It appears that I am the only one who has any idea how to *properly exercise* your power. I can hardly bear the injustice of it. But perhaps we can strike a deal," he offers with fake benevolence.

"I want to show you something. I want you to see my secret. I want to share."

Chapter 61

Wisty

THE ONE ESCORTS me into his private quarters, through the entryway I recognize from earlier. He slams the door shut, and I flinch, claustrophobic with the sense that I may never get out of here.

I glance at the desk across the room, remembering the private, sensitive documents in there, and suddenly feel cold down to my bones, as if I've stepped into a walk-in refrigerator. *Does he know?*

He guides me across the room, maneuvering me with his hand on the small of my back, and I feel sick. I had him, but curiosity got the better of me, and now I've let down my guard. I train my eyes straight ahead, looking at the unadorned walls, the small main room, unsure of what he has planned.

There's more to this place than I thought. He leads me to the far side of the room, to a spot in the wall that is slightly inconsistent, and I raise an eyebrow quizzically, but The One doesn't say a word. He lifts a hand, and a door flies open.

And I'm totally weirded-out by what lies behind it.

It's a seemingly endless hall of mirrors, and The One urges me forward, placing me in the middle to confront my own reflection. I half expect the mirrors to shatter at once, glass raining down on me in a dramatic finish, but all is still.

I peer into the mirrors, my image echoing into infinity, an army of Wistys looking small and scared and lost, just like I did in his bathroom. Looking weak. Then I remember the things I found there, the exposed vulnerability, and I set my jaw, determined not to let him get to me.

And when I change my expression, something happens.

A thousand Wistys mime this change back at me and stand there looking strong, confident, and so, so powerful. I feel the magic coursing through me, feel the truth of the Prophecies, and I *know*. I could rule this whole universe if I wanted to. It could all be mine.

I shudder, feeling light-headed.

"You see," The One whispers from behind me like a patient teacher coddling a wayward student, "it's not about you, Wisteria, and it's certainly not about *us,* or *we*. It's about me. It's about *I*. . . . The most powerful creative force, and the most dangerous, is the human ego. Now do you understand?"

Yes. I do understand.

Everything Mrs. Highsmith was trying to tell us about

power and playing God comes into acute focus. The important thing isn't about using The Gift; it's about *not* using it. About keeping others from getting ahold of it. Each one of us possesses that unique human narcissism, that self-importance that can spin wildly out of control, and the key to survival—to all of human survival—is keeping it under wraps.

"Power corrupts," I whisper. "Always remember."

I understand the enemy now. It's not just him, The One. It's *I*, me, *ego*, and I can't let that take over like this evil man has.

Chapter 62

Wisty

"SINCE WE'RE TALKING about ego...," I mutter to myself.

I turn to The One, keeping my eyes trained on his face and away from these warped mirrors.

"I understand now," I say. "But before I...join you...I want to know more about who you are, how you got here." I think back to the science award, the harsh teacher's note that I found earlier. Tools to get at him, to make him vulnerable. "Tell me how you got to be so..." I swallow. Say it like you mean it, Wist: *"Great."*

The One stands up a little straighter. Flattery suits him.

"Why, Wisteria, I told you I'd tell you anything— you just had to ask! It's only natural you should want to know how one could possibly achieve all that I have, that you should *covet* that power." His eyes flash at me, testing, but I nod at him as sincerely as I can manage, and he continues.

"Once upon a time, a small boy was...different. No,

not just different. Brilliant." He's speaking loudly now, as if performing for an audience, and his voice echoes through the tunnel of mirrors. "Those in a position of authority discouraged his immense talents, labeling him *hoodlum, ruffian, young terrorist*." The One's eyes glaze over as he recalls the memory. "Indeed, their assessment was astute on that account, for they would definitely endure terror," he mutters, then raises his voice. "Instead of helping him, encouraging him, they accused him of lies!"

" 'Disturbing demonstrations'?" I say before I can stop myself, recalling the paper I found in the desk, but The One doesn't seem to make the connection. Instead he nods, looking at me intently.

"Sound familiar? You and I are the same, Wisteria."

Is there any truth to that? I think back to my days of skipping school, of the disappointed looks around the dinner table, of everyone expecting me to fail because of the way I dressed or because I was smart in a different way than the other kids. It hurt. Still, that didn't make *me* take a hatchet to the whole world, did it?

"In what way are we the same?" Anger creeps into my voice. "I could *never* do what you do."

I look away from The One but only see his image reflected all around, and he takes a step closer, looming over me, his voice vibrating in my ears.

"Teachers, principals, your parents. They *failed* you. They never loved you, never appreciated the talent you possessed, never helped you hone it, grow it. Instead they wanted to squash it, kill it, to destroy you."

I think of my mom threading her fingers through my hair, my dad rocking out with me to a song on the radio, giving me a hard time about grades but giving me the space to be creative. Loving me, letting me be a kid instead of a prophet. Trying to protect me from this life of greed. How did The One get all of his power? Ego. Persuasion. Indoctrination. And a serious grudge against humanity.

"No." I shake my head, steeling my mind against The One's brainwashing. "It's you who's been trying to destroy me. *You*."

"Can't you see, child?" he asks, his voice dripping with false tenderness. "I've only wanted to be a good father to you, to give you the encouragement I never had. I'm invit- ing you to sit beside me. Everything I have" — he stretches his arms wide, and a thousand mirrored arms seem to reach for me, closing in — "could all be yours. I've only been trying to *help* the world, Wisty, to make them see. We only have to cleanse it of the useless and the pitiful, and then we can start anew. Come, I'll show you what you could have."

I can't even respond to that. One minute he's talking about trying to help the world, and in the same breath he proposes genocidal "cleansing"? What a sociopath.

Still, as The One walks to the end of the hallway, his thin frame guiding me along the mirrors, I follow. I'm in too deep to turn back now.

I realize I'm holding my breath, and when he turns the doorknob and presses forward, the hallway fills with warm, dazzling light.

And when I see what's inside that room, my head nearly explodes.

Chapter 63

Wisty

"NO...WAY," I whisper. My eyes bug out of my head, and I'm so dazed you could knock me over with a breath—even if you weren't The One.

Somehow, in this brick-and-mortar palace lies a door to a room that is infinite. It's bigger than a ballroom, a foolball field, a mall. I cannot see the far end, and as I press my hand against the golden walls to test if they're real (they are), my synapses are overloaded and my brain can process only one thought: *Beauty.*

On the walls and the floor, stacked in piles and leaning against corners, is *everything* that's been taken away from us. I stumble forward, breathlessly trailing my fingers against harps, guitars, centuries-old paintings by true masters. Light seems to emanate from these objects, drawing me in. All the greatest art, the greatest books, the greatest films, the greatest music, is right here. Every last thing.

Well, almost.

The collection we saw in Mrs. Highsmith's apartment was just a tiny fraction of what's in this room. It must have been what she hid from him, what she salvaged. She needed to save it for the rest of the world when the iron grip of the New Order had eased.

The One steps beside me and puts his hand on my shoulder, interrupting my thoughts.

"This is the good life, child, the only life worth living." He turns me toward him, holds my face in his hands, his thumbs pressing into my forehead, and I flinch. "You are superior. You should live a superior life. Look what you can share with me." My eyes flit to the stacks of music, the amplifiers, the sleekest guitar I've ever seen.

His thumbs press harder, and his eyes are wild, desperate. "Just give me your Gift. Give it to me."

Chapter 64

Wisty

AS HIS TECHNICOLOR eyes bore into mine, I finally see what he's capable of. It'll never end; it'll never be enough. One man's ego will leach all the life, all the beauty, from the whole world.

I think of all he's promised me, every lie, but my mind latches on to one statement made at his weakest moment: *You're doing it all wrong, Wisty. Backward,* he had said before, when I'd tried to pulverize him. What did he mean?

"Give it to me!" he shrieks over and over, pressing, pressing. I try to twist away, but he clenches my temples even harder. I'd do anything to make him stop.

And then...I understand.

If I can control electrical impulses of the brain...can I just stop them, too? Can I shut them down? Can I...kill someone? Just by concentrating on it?

Mrs. Highsmith said in no uncertain terms that I had to "deal with" The One.

Murder, she meant. A horrible, stifling guilt chokes me, but in that second, with The One's psychopathic eyes trained on me, I feel a lightning bolt strike between us. It lifts my feet right off the ground.

I don't know how I got here, or what to do.

But I don't know how to stop it either.

"No, Wisteria...," he gasps. "Not like that." His grip slides off, and he collapses to the floor. Panicked, I stand looking at his unconscious face, the white noise deafening in my ears.

I kneel down and slowly put my head on his chest, listening.

I'm shaking. I'm shaking and emotional and volatile, and I feel that familiar heat starting in my fingers. I stand up abruptly. I can't be here. Taking one last look around this paradise, I run past the artwork, past the guitars and sculptures with missing arms and noses, the girl on fire racing down the long, accusing hallway of mirrors.

Chapter 65

Wisty

I DON'T KNOW where I'm going, and I'm sobbing so hard I can barely see. I tear through the hall, down the stairs, into another hall of suites, not even feeling my legs carrying me.

And then I'm hit by a bus.

Well, that's what it feels like anyway.

Pearce has tackled me and rolled on top of me, and I hate myself for always finding him so attractive when I first see him. Luckily, every word that Pearce utters and every kid he tortures overrides that hormonal response to his bone structure pretty quickly.

"Is he *dead*?" Pearce shouts over me, eyes blazing. I stare into his face, unsure if he's hoping more for a yes or a no. He shakes my shoulders, slamming me into the floor. "Tell me, witch! Is he—?"

"No!" I yell back. "He's alive. He's still alive." I note his use of the word *witch*. "So you know that I'm..."

Pearce laughs like I'm the stupidest person in the Overworld. "Ah, yes, the infamous Wisteria Allgood, wanted fugitive." He grips my hair, and I turn away from his touch. "Even without your precious red hair, I was on to you. That's the weakest attempt at a disguise I've ever seen. I should've killed you when I had the chance, should've slaughtered you like a pig on that filthy floor."

"Why didn't you?" I challenge, fury building at remembering my humiliation in the barracks. "You were afraid of me, admit it."

"I didn't think you were worth it. But don't worry." His face is inches from mine, and his words drip with hatred. "I won't miss my chance this time. Believe me when I say that I want you dead even more than The One wants your Gift."

"The feeling is mutual, Pearce," I say, and he smirks.

"Glad we got to have a little foreplay first, though. Did it turn you on, Ms. Allgood? Did you find it... *hot*?"

"That wasn't my idea of hot... but *this* is!" Flames erupt from my body as if I'm doused in gasoline. I burn brightly, consumed with fury for this waste of a human being.

I shove him off me and scramble to hold him down, my fire licking at his face. He doesn't seem to be burning. He's not even sweating. I press in and Pearce rolls away, leaping up. I scramble after him to try to fight, but he's physically stronger than I am and he snatches my arm away.

And in that stunned moment, I realize my fire is having absolutely no effect. He's *immune*. He lunges in and grips my forehead, ready to melt my skull.

The brief second of contact is all I need.

Energy explodes between us, and I can instantly feel Pearce's synapses begin to shut down. His eyes roll back into his head, and foam starts to form at his mouth.

I'm killing him. Tears rush down my cheeks. *He's evil,* I remind myself. *He's a sadist who wants you dead.*

The door to the exit stairwell slams open, and as if in slow motion, I watch Byron running down the hall, his mouth frozen in one long *O*. Pearce's hand is still on my head. Byron has seen him liquefy a hundred kids' faces.

He thinks Pearce is killing me.

I put my hand up to flag him, but it's too late. Byron crashes into Pearce, and the connection is lost.

I snap out of my trance and rush over to Byron. He's still shouting furiously, and he doesn't let Pearce up like I expect him to—instead he punches him in the face over and over. I touch his shoulder, and his fist stops in midair.

"It's over, B. He's not getting up for a while." He looks at me, confused and emotional, like a little kid. He peers at his bloody fingers and doesn't seem to understand how they got that way.

"Come on," I say gently. "We have to go." He nods and we take off again, leaving Pearce bruised but breathing, slumped in a corner.

"I'm sorry, Wist," Byron says when we're beyond the compound. "I didn't understand what you were doing. That you were"—he looks away, swallowing—"going to kill him." He takes my hand. "I wouldn't have stopped you if I knew."

I shake my head. "I don't know if I could've finished it anyway. But we're in serious trouble now regardless."

Byron raises an eyebrow, questioning.

"Remember what happened at the music festival when I directed my energy through you?"

He nods. He'll never forget that.

"Well...I think I just made Pearce a whole lot stronger."

Chapter 66

Whit

WE RUN THROUGH the bone forest in single file, and even Feffer doesn't whine or make a sound. Celia swears the river can't be far, but as the air gets thinner and harder to breathe, I'm not sure we'll make it. Skeletons creak all around us, and arms seemingly come to life and reach for our bodies, wanting to absorb our life.

Even the trees are instruments of death.

There is sweat on my brow; I think I'm running a fever. My breath comes in short sips, and I can feel the magic seeping right out of me, draining my body.

Suddenly there's a spark flying off my fingertip, like I'm about to short-circuit or something. It's almost like my power is reacting to other forces here, all buzzing in this spot somehow, like too many wires plugged into one outlet.

The Shadowland seems to spiral as I hallucinate. I think I see a man's face in my vibrating vision—a face with sharp, jutting cheekbones and cruel eyes. Almost like The One's but... older. Warped. But when I blink it's only a tree skull, laughing at me. I'm losing my mind.

As if sensing my weakness, one of the younger Resistance kids catches up to me at the front, his skin sallow and his eyes ringed with dark circles. He's around twelve and has two even smaller children in tow.

"We're dying, aren't we?" The older kid looks at me with frank accusation, and I must seem bewildered. "The Shadowland is where the dead go, so we're about to die."

I close my eyes and try to get my composure together enough to reassure this kid, beaten by the world but surviving, and am unsure of what to say, how to tell him we'll get out of here, when I don't know for sure. "What's your name, kid?"

"Ragan," he says gruffly, a tuft of sandy-blond hair falling in his eyes. "Bennett Ragan."

"We're not dying, Ragan." Yet, at least. "The air here is just making us weak."

"Listen, I've been taking care of these two for a long time," he says, scowling. He grips the younger boys' hands in his. "I just want you guys to be honest with me."

As we near the edge of the forest, I'm feeling stronger again, less drugged. More optimistic. I put my hand on his shoulder. "I promise, if things get really bad, I'll give you a heads-up." Ragan nods, looking skeptical, and shuffles back to the end of the line.

As light finally breaks through the trees of the bone

forest, we stumble out onto a barren, rocky landscape with steep cliffs. We come to a clearing, a hilltop on the lip of what looks like a huge basin. What I see inside it sweeps my breath away for a moment.

In the valley below there are thousands of people, some flickering in and out of view, some with a dull half glow like Celia's.

Every single one of them is dead.

"This is the end of the world, Whit," Celia says. "I mean that literally. Your world ends right here. There, another world begins."

I start to race down the slope. If we're this close to so many dead people, the river can't be far.

And neither can my parents.

The rest of the Resistance follows me, rushing through the eerily lush green field toward our salvation.

"Wait!" Celia shouts, her voice trembling. "Not that way!" She turns and points at the path behind us. "They're coming," she whispers.

And then I see them, tearing over the hillside, teeth bared. Not dogs, exactly, or even wolves. *Beasts.*

Spirit-suckers—nonhuman Lost Ones. Flesh-eating fiends with the body of a beast and the mind of a demon.

I turn to Ragan. "I promised you I'd tell you if it was bad. Well, we're there. It's really, really bad. Run!"

But there's no time—they're already upon us.

Celia crashes into two of them, her bright light exploding against their evil, but though she's unharmed, they aren't afraid of her. They plow through her like air, and one seizes a kid from behind, snarling and thrashing. Celia is pleading in anguish, clawing at the animal's rank, rotting fur from behind, but she's too late.

A scream rips through the air, and I whip around to see a wolf tearing into Janine's shoulder. I run for her, but Feffer beats me there, lunging at the creature and distracting it from its feast. Feffer is no match for the beast, and she yips in pain as the soul-sucker bites at her legs and locks its jaws on her throat.

Wisty loved that dog.

I grab the closest object I can find — a bone — and rush toward them, arms raised. I strike a blow at the soul-sucker and it releases Feffer, lurching instead for me, its yellow eyes cold and calculating. It snaps at me with those long jaws, rows of teeth glistening, but I show no mercy, bashing the monster again and again as it roars at me furiously, until finally it collapses.

I kneel down to Janine's crumpled form and turn her over. She blinks up at me. Still breathing.

"Hey," I say, emotion warping my voice.

"Hey," she responds with a weak smile. "Good to see you."

I open up her shirt over her right shoulder, and she winces. The bite is a nasty gash, and the flesh there is shredded. But she'll live.

While war between man and beast rages all around us, I try to find calm to repair the damage. I put my hands on Janine's bloodied shoulder and wait for the power to surge through me, but my magic is only a flicker, the healing energy totally drained.

I drape Janine's arm around my neck and look around wildly for help, but most of the Resistance fighters are still engaged in to-the-death combat, and those who have managed to kill a soul-sucker or escape are far too weak now to help channel my power. Things are getting desperate.

We really are in hell.

Chapter 67

Wisty

THE STREETS ARE eerily quiet and free of guards as Byron and I sprint away from the palace. It's looking like a clean getaway, which is just about the only lucky thing that's happened to me in the last year.

It's still dark, but the street kids are already out en masse, their plastic garbage bags slung over their shoulders as they pick through the streets for anything left by the careless rich. The competition is cutthroat, and once they realize we don't have a bean between us they don't pay us any mind.

A black dog noses around in the garbage in the dim light of the alley, and my heart aches for Feffer. The dog's ragged ears prick up at the distant howl of a pack of N.O. hunting wolves, and his tail goes between his legs.

We're barely out of the range of the wolves and search-lights before Byron is wheezing like an asthmatic eighty-year-old smoker after a workout. I notice my own exhaustion for the first time. It's either keep going or collapse at this point.

"Do you have *any* idea where we're headed anyway?" I ask. I probably would have preferred to ditch the weasel if I wasn't totally turned around in this maze of N.O. concrete. Without him, I'm sure I'd end up stumbling right back through the palace-compound gates.

Byron coughs, hands on his knees. "Of course I know where we're going," he says indignantly. "There's a portal I know of, a top secret, intensely complicated gateway that few of the most elite N.O.P.E. members even know about. It leads to the darkest, most terrifying part of the Shadowland." Byron looks at me gravely.

Sure, going to the Shadowland always involves a certain amount of risk and trepidation, but the guy can be *so* dramatic.

"And your intel says that's where Whit's hanging out?"

"Well, the information is less specific than we'd hope for" (Byron code for *No, I'm taking a wild guess here and hope I'm right*) "but there's evidence to suggest that Whit is highly sought after by the dead, and one can assume that he would be drawn to the more remote areas in his quest to locate your parents," he reports.

"Headed for the worst place at the worst possible time? Yeah, that sounds like my brother." I try to smile, but Byron's probably right, actually. A tightness closes around my heart. *Please let Whit be okay.*

Byron sighs. "And we're on a deadline. The report said,

'The end is near,' whatever that means, so we need to find Whit as soon as possible."

I nod. The end has felt near for a very long time.

"And, Wist? There's another thing I suspect you're not going to be rather ecstatic about."

Another thing? As in, worse than "the end is near"? I cock an eyebrow, and Byron hesitates.

"What? Just say it."

"The portal is not exactly easy to get through — because it's underwater."

Underwater. My hands start to sweat and my throat goes dry remembering the claustrophobic nightmare of being flushed through the sewer (in fish form) not so very long ago. Great — I'm sure this will be a thrill a minute.

"If I can handle The One, I think I can manage a little aqua," I say mildly, but I feel a chill at his words. "The sun's starting to come up. Can we just get going already?"

We run for a few more blocks through the rubble of the streets, the cement buildings towering around us like vultures closing in. Byron signals left, and when we turn, a river is just up ahead of us, bisecting the City of Progress.

Dawn breaks over the water as we approach, and the pink glow makes our ravaged capital look almost beautiful. If I didn't expect to be shot at any second, if I were a normal girl in normal circumstances, I'd sit right down on this curb and watch as the sun edged up over the horizon.

"The portal." Byron nods at the river, snapping me back to reality. I am not a normal girl, after all. Not anymore.

I want to immediately take off toward the portal and find my brother, but something makes me hesitate—something more than just paranoia about the water. There's an uncomfortable eeriness that I can't pinpoint. There are no people out anymore, and the bean-picker children have disappeared completely. No birds, no wind, and the river is barely stirring. The air is still.

Too still.

"B., does something feel . . . off . . . to you?"

He eyes the clouds looming above us, unmoving, jaundiced yellow and pregnant with threat. "Uh, yeah. You could say that."

A strong wind is already picking back up, and the sky is going dark in a hurry. Byron grabs my hand and we dash forward toward the portal, but the once calm streets turn swiftly into a nightmare of flying debris, and the river's waves become crashing, deadly rapids. It's like a hurricane spinning into a tornado.

Amid the chaos, waves of soldiers start to pour in from the side streets with the wind at their backs. I freeze. It's not possible: Pearce, racing at the helm, his strong jaw set with determination, his fair, wavy hair trailing behind him in the violent wind.

And—worse—The One by his side, his face wild with power, lust, and . . . something else. Fury.

How have they healed so quickly? I left them both weak

and wounded, but now Pearce and The One take command of the swirling skies, a mega-power looms large above us, and nothing has ever felt stronger.

Including my fear.

Byron is tugging on my arm, shielding his eyes from the wreckage, but I just stand there, mouth gaping, utterly overwhelmed. The wind whips my long hair and rain batters my face, but I can't seem to move an inch.

Both The One's and Pearce's eyes are burning white-hot, united with a particular, undisguised hatred for The Fire Girl, The One With The Gift.

The girl who tried to kill them and might have succeeded.

The girl who will pay dearly for her sins.

A mass of dread forms in my stomach, and my body is shaking all over. This is surely my worst nightmare come for me at last.

Chapter 68

Whit

THE SHARP, METALLIC scent of blood hangs in the air, and the hill is crowded with human and animal bodies.

I spot Ragan picking over the injured, desperation on his face. He looks okay, but as he kneels next to a silent, unmoving form, gathering it up into his arms, I know we haven't made it through without any losses. The smallest of Ragan's two charges is next to him, crying. Celia joins them and wraps her arms around the boy, rocking him as he weeps for his brother.

I feel something harden inside me, and tears don't come. I've seen it all before—orphaned, trusting kids hacked out of existence while trying to find their way home. I think of Pearl Marie's voice as she talked about Ziggy, and guilt lodges in my gut like a stone. What was I doing making promises to that kid?

Janine looks at Ragan and then turns her face against

my chest, shutting out the scene. Her arm hangs limply at her side, red blooming through her shirt.

Holding her here on this eerily lush, green hillside surrounded by the macabre reality, I feel like a character on a page ripped from a book, where there's no time and no ending, no way to move forward.

I look over Janine's head into the valley below, seeing the ghostly beings moving around down there, watching us. Expecting…what? Then, just beyond the ambling dead, where the red haze has dissipated the tiniest bit, something sparkles. I put a hand up to shield my eyes, squinting, and think I can make out a thin gray line moving, reflecting the light.

The river, I mouth, realization dawning on me. The very same river from the vision at Mrs. Highsmith's apartment — the one where I saw my parents. I motion to the others, pointing. I know we should be celebrating; we finally made it. But when Ragan looks over at me, his eyes swollen and his face bitter, I can only think, *At what cost?*

Celia comes up behind us. She puts her hand on my back and rests her head on my shoulder.

"You think my mom and dad are down there, Celia?" I ask, squinting at the crowd.

She smiles sadly, still shaken. "I don't know for sure, but I'll help you look. Come on."

Celia takes my hand, and Janine's as well. She turns to the others, scattered on the hillside. Sasha and Emmet nod and start across the uneven ground toward us, shoulders heavy, but most of the kids aren't budging.

"I know it's hard, and I know you're all hurting, but we can't stop now," I call.

"*Another* battle?" Sasha says, limping over. "Haven't we been through enough? No offense, but I'm sick of being dragged along and almost killed for your sake. I just want to get us all out of here."

Some of the other kids nod in agreement, but Janine speaks up.

"Whit is one of us," she says sharply, cradling her arm. "We're fighting for him, but we're fighting for the Resistance, too. Have you forgotten why we ended up here in the first place? There's no safe haven in the Overworld until we face the battles in the Underworld. Would you rather just give up now after coming this far?"

Sasha sighs, the public scolding obviously stinging him a bit.

My heart swells with respect for Janine. I know the pain from her shoulder is worse than she's letting on, but she always has a fighting spirit.

The rest of the kids reluctantly join the group. The only way out of this nightmare is through it, it seems. Together we look toward the thin river of hope calling to us, promising salvation.

Chapter 69

Wisty

"THIS WILL BE the end of you, girl," The One howls over the wind, his arms spread out like a maestro directing the scene as he levitates above the violent eye of the storm. "I can promise you that much. Are you ready to be nothing but a memory—and then not even that?"

Pearce has instructed the troops to block all exit routes, and he strides toward me along the bank, pretentiously flanked on either side by elite N.O. guards, the whites of his wicked eyes flashing furiously at me.

"I think so," I whisper numbly. Maybe I *am* ready to be done with all of this.

The clouds race across the heavens faster, and the massive, whirling twister towers above me, just a slight girl battling the whole sky. I open my arms, palms up, a lamb offered for the slaughter, and a deafening clap of thunder bellows its response.

I concentrate on the last sensations I will possibly ever

experience, feel the hard rain tearing across my face and sense the cold wind on my eyelids, my tangled hair whipped in the raging gale. I hear the roar of the storm as it grows in strength, but my ears strain to hear something else as well.

Byron. I'd forgotten him.

"Wisty, *come right now!* You can get away!" he bellows.

I snap open my eyes to see a spectacular flash of lightning strike nearby, and in a magical dance of luck, timing, and sheer adrenaline, I'm able to instantaneously send all my electrical energy into manipulating it.

Debris swirls around us as I hurl the supercharge at The One and his soldiers. The flashing crackle flies from my fingers and finds its target: the river, with the New Order troops all wading through the shallow water. The connection lights up the sky, and for a moment hundreds of men convulse like marionettes as electricity shoots through their bodies.

I feel nauseous. Those were men with families, with hopes. But they were also men who'd done unspeakable things, I remind myself, who'd performed experiments on children and executed their parents.

But is there ever an excuse for mass murder?

I glimpse The One's face, distorted with anger and... what else? Admiration? And I hear Pearce's enraged yelling behind him, but then I turn away from them, toward the turbulent river. Toward the Shadowland, and my parents.

Now is the moment when terror finally grips my heart. But there's no time to think of drowning, to imagine my lungs exploding.

Instead I inhale a giant gulp of air, and Byron grabs my hand as we plunge into the deep, swirling frenzy of water. I kick my feet fiercely and don't stop until we push through a portal and deep into the Shadowland.

Chapter 70

Whit

THE RIVER OF Forever is not the serene, clear-blue comfort that you'd hope to greet your soul after you've exhaled your last breath in the Overworld. Instead it's a gray mass of angry, roiling waves, ominous and forbidding, surrounded by the anarchy of the dead.

But it's as if the water has a magnetic pull, too; I stumble toward it as if hypnotized. As I near, I can see an ancient-looking drawbridge firmly locked in a raised position. Who knows how long it's been that way? There's a mass of accumulated souls throwing themselves into those furious waters, but they can't cross. Instead, the river rolls them violently about, tossing them like limp fish back onto the bank. I feel an overwhelming need to jump, too, along with a vague panic at the thought of not being able to control that urge. Celia puts her hand on my arm, shaking her head in warning.

Sasha has taken Ragan and some of the others to rest

away from the crowds, but a few of us, including Janine and Celia, have started elbowing through the masses along the bank, trying to find the spot on the river where I remember seeing my parents, in the vision at Mrs. Highsmith's.

It's chaotic, with lines snaking back and forth and mobs of the newly dead wandering aimlessly through this antechamber of the afterlife, and no one seems to be able to help us. Some people are weeping, but most are dazed and in shock, nearly unresponsive.

"They don't get that they're dead," Celia explains, nodding at a group of older people huddled together near us, confused and terrified. "They're not like the Half-lights—not like me. They don't have...unfinished business." She smiles sadly. "But until they cross the River of Forever, a lot of them just don't understand what's going on."

"And is it always like this?" I can't believe that this frenzied mass of people is always so immense and confused. This *can't* be how it's supposed to go.

Celia's brow creases. "I don't know, Whit. You expect me to know everything about this place, and I just *don't!*" I'm momentarily stunned by her anger. Celia never snaps—at me or anyone.

I try to squeeze her hand, wanting reassurance that it's fine; we're fine. I forgot I wouldn't be able to feel it. It's like grasping at air. It seems like now that we're physically the closest we've been since she disappeared from the Overworld, strangely she feels farthest away. How can we truly understand each other when we've had such intense experiences on our own?

She sighs. "I'm sorry, okay? It's just that I've been trying to get across that river just like everyone else for as long as I've been here. You can feel it pulling, can't you?"

I nod. It's an effort to keep myself on solid ground.

"I feel that pull every second, all the time."

"I'm sorry," I say quietly. "It must be hard."

She presses her lips together and looks out at the gray waves. "I don't think this is the way it's supposed to be, but this is all I know: Some of the other Half-lights have heard rumors that The One's power has leaked into the Shadowland and it's just screwing with everything, but we're all guessing. The only thing I know for sure is that until balance is restored, we're stuck on this side, and the dead just keep coming."

"Maybe that means that it's not final, then," Janine suggests. "That . . . the dead aren't really dead yet."

"But they are," Celia says testily. "Just look at them."

I peer at the bewildered faces of those around us. In their frightened, yearning eyes, the spark has unmistakably been extinguished. There is no light here, no *life*. Which means that if my parents are here, they really are just like these people. . . .

Dead.

The thought takes my breath away, and the ground whirls under me. I sit down abruptly, head in my hands.

"Whit!" Celia crouches next to me, alarmed. She probably

wants to see me as the guy I used to be, too — this big-shot quarterback, invulnerable and easygoing. But I can't be that guy for her right now. Not anymore.

Not in this world.

"I just..." I search her face, my head swimming. "I never believed it. I always held out the hope that they'd be alive somewhere, somehow. But if my parents are here, then they're..."

Celia nods, rubbing my back, though I can't feel it. "Then they're like me."

I stand up. Whatever the outcome, whatever the state of my parents, I've come this far and I have to find them. I look around at the mob, eager for a familiar face.

And I see one — but not the one I expect.

He's a bit younger than I am, slightly built, with bushy dark hair standing out from his head in all directions. Half of his face is missing.

Daniel Anderson. I knew him in high school — he was in Wisty's class, I think.

I went to his funeral.

The whole school was there, the girls all sobbing, the guys stone-faced but some of them crying a little, too. His girlfriend — a pinch-faced sophomore cheerleader, a girl Celia never got along with — talked about how much he liked video games and his car. As she said it, his mother got hysterical.

It was the car that killed him.

He was the first person I ever *really* knew who'd died.

They called it a tragedy. That was before the New Order, before any of us understood what tragedy was.

"Daniel." I put my hand on his shoulder, and he whirls around, jumpy, scared.

"I don't understand," he murmurs. "Is it time?" he asks, and I try not to stare at the crater in the left side of his head. His eyes widen as if he's seen the future in my face. He's looking at me like the Lost Ones did, with desperation and crushing hope.

"Save me," he pleads. *"Please."*

I back away from him, suddenly on my guard, but his cavernous eyes follow me, expectant. "I will," I say, though I have no idea how. "I promise . . . I promise I'll do whatever I can."

Then Janine whispers in a very small voice, "Save me, too, Whit." She's leaning heavily on Emmet now, and I can see how shallow her breathing is. The blood has soaked her shirt a sticky dark brown. Her face is almost translucent, and a cold sweat stands out on her brow.

I nod solemnly.

I don't know how I'll manage it, but I need to save her more than anything.

Chapter 71

Wisty

IT'S SO DARK in this part of the Shadowland that Byron and I can't see a thing in front of us. We have no idea where we are, where we're going, or where my brother is. We're picking our way over uneven, rocky ground, and I can just barely make out the reaching branches of a pocket of trees up ahead.

There's magic over there, I can feel it, like some kind of cocktail of dark energy pulling my own M toward it. I stray from the path to take the quickest way possible toward those alluring trees and immediately slam my shin into a boulder in the darkness.

"Wisty—watch out! Careful!" Byron urges.

Why the heck do people always tell you to watch out *after* you're already hurt?

The gash is wet with blood, and I bite my lip, stifling a cry, and Byron holds my hand in support. After a minute the pain ebbs and I stand up, ready to set out again. Even though I'm kind of disturbed that Byron is still holding my hand in his clammy grip, I'm too scared to let go.

"At least we're safe here," I say, trying to look on the bright side.

"Safe?" Byron repeats. "You neglect to account for flesh-eating Lost Ones and spirit-suckers, not to mention the danger of getting trapped in this maze forever and eventually running out of strength . . . and oxygen."

I can always count on Byron for a healthy dose of optimism.

"*Relatively* safe, I mean. Safe from Pearce and The One. They're Straight and Narrows, right? So we don't have to deal with them in the Shadowland, at least."

Byron conspicuously doesn't answer.

My skin is still wet from the river, and my dripping hair makes it feel like I'm crawling with a thousand roaches, their little legs scurrying over my arms and down my neck. And now Byron's got me thinking about Lost Ones. After ten minutes of stumbling along in the pitch-blackness, paranoid, I've had about enough of the creepy quiet and dark.

"All right, Byron, say something annoying." I've lost count of the times when I've flamed out in a Byron-induced rage.

"What? Wisty, after all we've been through, I resent that you would imply—"

"Just kidding. I've got it pretty much down to a science at this point. Stand back."

As he lets go of my hand, I release a spark, and suddenly I'm covered in the familiar glow, flames licking out from my body.

I *love* the feeling of being a human torch.

"Whoa," Byron breathes, and I still feel a bit of pride at the awe in his voice. "That seriously never gets old."

I lead the way down a path full of potholes, along craggy cliffs. Insects crunch and slither beneath our feet, and I shudder. Was it really my wet hair that I felt crawling on me?

"Where are we going anyway?" Byron asks after a few minutes.

"I don't know. To the end, I guess. Didn't you say that the end is near? I think you might be right, B."

I mean it as a joke, but it comes out way more serious, and Byron goes quiet.

I kind of feel sorry for the guy. True, he has a history of playing both sides and hasn't always been 100 percent trustworthy, but this particular time it *is* kind of my fault he's part of the focus of a cross-world manhunt. And he did think he was saving my life back there with Pearce. I sigh.

"Listen, Byron, I meant to tell you..." I cough. I'm really bad at this. "I'm uh...sorry...for, you know, turning you into a weasel. Even if you did deserve it."

Byron's eyes cloud over—with tears? Okay, I wasn't prepared for *that*.

"Hey, now," I mumble uncomfortably. "No need to get

all emotional. I just wanted to let you know that despite all the bad blood between us in the past, I'm starting to think you're a pretty solid guy. Maybe even...a friend." His lip quivers, and I wag a finger in warning. "Not that I'm not prepared to revoke that judgment if the situation calls for it."

He nods vigorously but is still fighting back a sob. This is totally awkward.

"I will *never* let you down again, Wisty. I know I've said some things in the past, but...I just think you're amazing, and you don't know what it means to me to hear"—he sniffles—"to have your friendship, I mean. I swear that you can depend on my allegiance and expect the highest level of commitment in the future and—"

I put up a hand. "Okay, got it, Byron. No need to go overboard, just...c'mere."

I let the flame extinguish for a second and hold my arms out tentatively for a totally platonic, not-weird-in-any-way, tiny hug of friendship. Byron practically leaps at me, squeezing me half to death and probably getting snot and tears and God knows what else in my hair.

Still, the whole thing is kind of heartwarming, and I can't help being a bit relieved.

Chapter 72

Whit

WE, THE LIVING, are bloodied, weak, and struggling to breathe the air in this wretched place. But as we shuffle in a line through the crowds milling along the river—Sasha and Emmet, wounded but defiant, Ragan with his surviving young charge, Janine and I—we positively radiate *life* against this backdrop of dead.

Well, all of us except Celia. We follow her Half-light through the sea of spirits, to a group of more people I know—or knew. People from our town. People who might be able to help us locate my parents.

"Have you seen Benjamin and Eliza Allgood?" I ask no one in particular, trying to shift their focus. "Please—has anyone seen my parents?" I ask more forcefully.

"Whit!" Sasha waves me over to a stooped spirit.

The man is ancient, with papery skin. He's draped in a flowing black robe. I don't recognize him at first, but without warning he leans in and gives me a stiff, very cold hug.

He smells sour, but there's something else there, too: the faint smell of cinnamon.

Memories flood back to me as I realize that I know this man, too: it's the old minister from the church that our parents used to take us to, when we were little kids, back when religion was legal. We stopped going when Wisty and I were pretty young, but it's him, all right.

He mumbles something that I can't understand, and I lean in closer, eager for direction.

"Can you bear it, son?" he croaks. "Can you bear to witness the truth?" Then he points a spindly finger. I hold my breath as I follow it with my eyes, and Celia grips one of my trembling hands, Janine the other.

My feet are carrying me forward before my brain even registers the scene. Down the banks of the River of Forever, there is a couple, a man and a woman, working their way through the crowds of people, lining them up, organizing them, comforting them.

"Mom! Dad!" I shout midstride. Their heads turn to look at me, and emotion rips through my chest.

It's really them.

"Whit?" my mom gasps, her voice part hope, part anguish. I reach her first and swing her into a fierce embrace.

"Mom, I thought I'd never—" My voice breaks off. I have to stop talking or I'll lose it.

She's so, so thin. Emaciated. Her arms encircle me, but I can barely feel her. It's as if I'm being hugged by a ghost.

But I *can* feel her. She has *substance,* even just a little, and the spark in her eyes burns so, so bright when she looks into mine.

A sob catches in my throat, and my whole body shudders as I grip my mother in my arms with every bit of my strength.

I'm not sure how long I'm clutching her before I spot a man behind her whom I hardly recognize. He's aged a hundred years and seems shrunken, slight.

"Dad?" I whisper, unbelieving. I untangle myself from Mom's arms and run to meet the man who has always been my rock, my solid ground. The man I thought I'd lost forever.

He grips me in a ferocious hug, and his arms are stronger than ever. Strong and *solid*.

I can feel both of my parents.

Which means...*Are they dead or alive?* I can't bear to ask that question, so I ask the next-best one. I pull away from my dad and look from him to Mom, needing to know.

"What is this river? And what are you guys doing here?"

Mom's voice is soft, coaxing, like when she tried to help me with a difficult math problem in my homework when I was a kid. "You know what it is, Whit. It's the river to the other side."

"And what's on the other side?" I ask stubbornly.

"We all find out in our own time," my dad says. "Whit, *this* is the most important time in your and Wisty's lives. The world is in terrible upheaval, and the backup at the river is just a symptom of it. We never dreamed it would happen this way, this quickly."

"What exactly *is* happening?" I demand. Despite how relieved I am to see my parents, I find myself angry with them, too. They *should* have prepared us better. And they're still feeding me these half-truths.

Mom holds my hand as if she never wants to let it go. "The One Who Is The One has raised the bridge across the River of Forever, and chaos has erupted. The natural flow of life, of fate, of the Prophecies, has been critically interrupted."

"Very soon we'll find out if the Prophecies will or will not be fulfilled," Dad jumps in. "But Wisty is as much a part of it as you are." He puts his hands on my shoulders, his voice pleading. "Whit, where is your sister?"

"I have no *idea* where she is," I say, exasperated. "Why don't you ask your friend Mrs. Highsmith? She's the one who said Wisty had to deal with The One. She's the one who sent each of us off on our own. But right now it all seems nothing short of insane. I should've never trusted that old lady. I don't even want to think about what could've happened to Wisty."

I feel a pang as I get the words out and instantly regret it when I see my parents' faces sag. I'd been trying to focus on just what was in front of me. The truth is, I'm crazy with worry about my little sister.

"Mom, Dad, I..." I put a hand on Mom's wrist.

"She's here," Celia cuts in. "I feel it somehow. It's like

her light, her fire, is changing the energy of this place. She's in the Shadowland. I'm sure."

Dad beams at Celia, but my mom's brow creases. "Time is running out, though."

Celia looks scared. "I know. I'm not sure she'll be able to get here in time."

"This is exactly what The One wanted," Dad says angrily, realizing the implications. "If he gets to Wisty in the Shadowland, and gets to her alone...it could be the end...of everything."

"What do you mean, *the end of everything*?" I ask.

A look passes between my parents and Celia. What do they know?

"What's supposed to happen?" I press, but they won't meet my eyes.

I've had it with the meaningful looks meant for only the all-knowing dead. I've had it with secrecy. I know that my sister is important in all of this, and that she's in an absurd amount of danger, and that's all I really need to know. If she's here, I'll find her.

I turn away from all of them and take off at a clip.

"Whit!" my father calls after me.

"I'm going to find her," I call over my shoulder. "I've looked out for Wisty my whole life, and I'm not going to stop now."

Chapter 73

Wisty

BYRON AND I barrel through the mazelike turns of the Shadowland, desperately trying to make it to Whit and my parents before this so-called end of everything.

We're deeper into the Shadowland than I've ever been before, and the lightening sky isn't a comfort when the clouds are bloodred and the forest seems carnivorous. The trees, which appear to be made of ... bone? ... lurch toward us, whispering things I can't decipher. I stop for a second, ears perked up.

"What is it?" Byron asks, but I shake my head. I can't explain why, but I feel like I can hear Celia's musical voice echoing through the hollow passage, and I can sense my brother, as if he had been here not long ago.

"Nothing, I just think we're on the right path."

Just then, a bone snaps behind us, and I jump a mile high. Byron lets out a yelp, which doesn't exactly defuse the tension.

A low chuckle erupts at our expense. I whip around to see Pearce, calm and striking, blond head leaning against a tree, gazing with fascination at his prey.

My whole body tenses. I try to block it, but the kiss Pearce forced on me flashes in my mind again. Now just the sight of him evokes both shame and seething rage.

"You may indeed have been on the right path to find your family, Ms. Allgood. It's a shame you'll never reach them now," he says almost apologetically.

I turn to Byron. "Pearce is a *Curve?*" I whisper harshly, jabbing him in the ribs.

Byron grimaces and rubs his temples. "I probably should've told you, but I wasn't sure. He's younger than most of the N.O. soldiers and highly perceptive, so I suspected he might be."

Pearce smiles with smug satisfaction. "You don't do me justice, Swain. I wasn't just a Curve, but a former N.O.P.E. officer, no less. Not that it matters anyway, since The One Who Is The One has now breached the final frontier."

The realization blows my mind. "The One is in the Shadowland?" I murmur. *The end.* That's what the rumor meant. "How...?"

"Oh, I'd guess that you helped him out with your little power surge back at the palace." Pearce chucks a bone at a tree across the path with surprising force, and it snaps cleanly in two. I'm guessing he hasn't forgotten the power surge I gave *him* either.

He grins, and his sparkling white teeth look positively

deadly. "But, regardless, The One has surely reached the rest of the Allgood family by now." He cocks his head. "You remember watching your dear parents go up in smoke, don't you, Wisty?" The pain hits me like a jolt of electricity, and my hands ball into fists.

"Of course I remember," I say through clenched teeth.

Pearce looks off into the distance, gesturing at a fake scene with his hands. "Well, imagine, if you will, your helpless parents and your weak joke of a brother being truly vaporized this time, from the Shadowland to the depths of hell." He looks at his wrist as if checking the time. "That should be happening...right about now."

That's when I hurl myself at him.

Byron panics and tries to hold me back, but I'm practically foaming at the mouth.

"Wisty, you can't!" He tugs at my arms. "Don't make him stronger! Let me fight!"

I cast a glance at this scrawny guy, so hopeful, so reckless, such a good friend. "No, B. We'll do it together," I tell him.

"Oh, this should be good." Pearce laughs. "The princess and the toad, joining forces. All right, then. Here we go."

Pearce walks up the tree as if unbound by gravity, then pushes off and pounces toward us, catlike. I duck, but he manipulates the wind to raise me up and catches me in the face with a stinging backhand. It hurts, but I know it's just a fraction of what he's capable of.

He's playing with us.

I try to focus my power, but then he just...disappears.

The air ripples behind us, and I dodge out of the way as Pearce materializes, but he's already swiped a boot under Byron's leg, sending him careening to the ground.

"I could kill you right now, of course, but you guys are just so much *fun*." He laughs, watching Byron scramble off the floor.

I snatch Byron's hand and center all of my power through our connection, a raging, deadly ball of energy circulating through our fingertips and searing into Pearce.

"You *still* don't get how this works, do you?" Pearce hovers above us, unfazed. "Tell me, how is it possible that the Prophecy could revolve around someone so imbecilic? You've made The One stronger, made *me* stronger. Every time you use your 'Gift' "—he makes air quotes—"on us, we take a little more and you get weaker. You. Can't. Win."

My anger fuels another astonishing burst of fuel through Byron and me, and Pearce winces. Light erupts around us, and I can feel the supernaturally powerful electrical current surging, stinging, smoking.

But though I may be ten times stronger than I've ever been, though we're zapping Pearce with a current far more potent than what almost killed him at the palace, he's... right.

He's stronger than we are. Still.

The realization hits me right as Pearce throws one of my own currents right back in our direction. The jolt tears through us, and Byron flies backward, ripped from my grasp. He lies twenty feet from me, his body twisted at appalling angles. Unmoving.

With the connection lost, I'm weaker than ever and can't fend off this monster any longer. I try to scramble away, but he grabs at my hair with one hand, wrenching me backward and off my feet.

Pearce starts to get his claws around my head, and I wince, bracing for the end.

Chapter 74

Whit

MY TIMING IS perfect. I see Wisty caught in Pearce's death grip, and alarm bells explode in my head. I'm seeing red.

I streak toward them from the woods and slam my whole body into Pearce with the force of a thousand rabid soul-suckers, pounding him to the ground. He's wickedly strong, but in that moment he's no match for my absolute need to save my sister.

He's down, but probably not for long.

I rush over to Wisty, crumpled on the forest floor. Relief sweeps through me as I realize my sister is alive. She's coughing and choking on the ground and she's got a nasty welt on the side of her cheek, but she's alive.

"Hey." Wisty eyes me, pain written all over her face. "I was wondering when you'd show up. Not that I didn't" — she collapses in a coughing fit — "have the situation under control."

"Shh," I tell her. "Take it easy." But as I rub my sister's back, I'm filled with debilitating fury. I survey the situation and see the pale, bloodied form of Byron Swain curled lifelessly against a stump.

I feel the color drain from my face. No one deserves to go out like this.

"Don't. Move," I sneer as Pearce starts to get up, iron in my voice. "I'll kill you where you stand."

Pearce smiles, jovial as ever behind those cold eyes. "Let me get this straight: *You're* telling *me* not to move? I don't think you quite understand who's in charge of this situation here, whiz kid." His eyes flash a warning. "Or who is going to be the one to die."

I stand up and move away from Wisty, keeping on the balls of my feet, keeping ready.

"You forget that we don't have to fear you, Pearce. You can't kill us. The One wants us alive, otherwise he can't take our magic. You're the only vulnerable party here." I try not to look at Byron's mangled body off to the side.

Pearce laughs. "Ah, Whit. Naive, sensitive, idiotic Whitford Allgood. It may amuse you to learn that I've discovered a way to absorb your magic, actually. The only thing it requires is...your death. The thing is, if I kill you, I'll grow even stronger. Then the only part left to do—and I'm really sad you're going to miss out on this—will be to bring your beloved sister back to The One to do the honors of the slaughter."

His face changes, and I see that he's got his own agenda behind that loyal mask. "That is, if I feel like it. I don't really need his assistance at all anymore, if we're being honest."

Chapter 75

Whit

MY HANDS ARE balled into fists, but sweat still pools in my palms as we maneuver around each other.

As I step over Byron's motionless body—one arm still flung across his head protectively, the other reaching for my sister—I feel such hatred for Pearce that I'm surprised I'm not the one shooting fire.

He is going to pay.

I'm angry but not stupid. I try to keep my distance from him at first, crouching low and moving slowly through the eerie red light, anticipating his first move. He's uncharacteristically silent, which puts me even more on edge.

Considering our last encounter, I expected Pearce to be afraid of me, or at least to show some respect. Instead he exudes confidence with that taunting little smile. He stays on the offensive, his long strides pushing me farther and farther into the woods, where the volume of magic is increasingly oppressive.

I'm dizzy before the fight even starts.

Soon the path narrows, the arms of the bone trees reaching for us like hungry demons. He's got me backed into a corner. I've beaten Pearce before, but I'll be honest, there's no way I can take his being anywhere near my skull again. If I close my eyes, I can almost still feel the white-hot pain searing through my temples.

I look at this kid with his sociopathic stare, and my hands go cold, my pulse thundering in my ears. I'm confronted by my oldest enemy: Fear.

Then I remember my injured sister and my dead friend lying on the ground among the roaches and bones, and I lunge at the snake with a heart full of vengeance.

I've got him beaten on physical strength and bulk alone, but he moves quickly and athletically, effortlessly dodging most of the punches I throw. He must've taken my last "mano a mano" challenge to heart, because I'm seriously paying for it now. He clearly has extensive military combat under his belt, and soon I'm dripping with sweat and breathing hard.

The magic in this place is making me weaker, my punches clumsy. How stupid was I not to think about how this forest affected me the last time?

Pearce catches me in the side, and I stumble off the path into a tree, coming face-to-face with a decaying, grinning skull that snaps its jaws. When I turn from it in horror, Pearce is already coming at me again with a jaunty, almost playful step, and I finally start to realize that the odds are not in my favor here.

He seems vastly stronger now than he was before. He may be an arrogant jerk with delusions of grandeur, but when he says he doesn't need The One's help anymore, I believe him.

Which means I'm a bit overmatched.

I get lucky and nail him with a crushing hook to the jaw that should've downed him, but somehow he stays upright.

Pearce takes advantage with a jab in my stomach, quick and vicious. I bend at the waist with a shocked groan, and by the time I suck in a wheezing breath of sour air, he's spun me into a deadly choke hold.

All I can think is *You are a star athlete, Whit. How did this even happen?*

I'm going to die here today.

And then he's going to kill my little sister before she even gets to see our parents again.

I kick and flail, shoving my elbows into him, my face puffing up with the strain, but I can't seem to break free from his grasp.

"Now, now, hold *still*, Whitford. This'll only hurt for a second." He laughs cruelly. "Okay, that's not really true."

I'm almost unconscious, and at first I think he's going to melt my face, but that doesn't seem to be on the agenda.

He's suddenly grabbing my legs, *compressing them* all the way up to my stomach—no, *into* my stomach. My organs are being crushed. Imagine being disemboweled with your own body parts, the agony vibrating from both sides, and you might be close to where I'm at right now.

Looks like Pearce has been practicing a new death trick.

What information can I give him to make him stop? my mind screams. But of course I don't have any, and he wouldn't anyway.

And it just gets worse.

I can't say what's happening, but in every single cell of my body I feel the most excruciating pain, as if he's forcing my limbs and torso inside my own skull, creating a human *foolball* of me. I can see his hands, but that's all. I am beyond thought. I can only watch in horror as Pearce points a finger into the distant wilderness of the Shadowland.

"Go long!" he shouts to Wisty, whom I can't see, though I can hear her pitiful begging, her useless sobs. "No? No matter. I'm sure one of the bone trees will catch him."

And then my compressed body is falling from his hands, only to connect with his steel-toed boot in a vicious dropkick that sends me sailing through the air. It's all I can do not to howl. Instead I focus my strength on absorbing the blow, on reversing the spell, on...anything but the inevitable.

The world turns itself inside out and back again as I spin through the air, barreling closer and closer to one of those mammoth trunks at astonishing speed, a car facing a head-on collision. *Oh no.*

No, no, no...

My skull smashes into a bone tree with the force of a freight train, but I don't shatter. I don't die.

I *bounce*.

As I whip through the air, my body is forced back out of the skull ball with seemingly no broken bones or permanent damage.

I'm alive, but I've never been more freaking ticked off in my life.

I hurl myself forward, rage distorting my features and my vision. I have time only to see the astonished look on Pearce's stupid mug before I plow into his chest, clawing and thrashing at eighty miles an hour.

Safe to say he's down for the count.

Chapter 76

Wisty

"WE SHOULD'VE CHECKED," I mumble to my brother. "We should've made sure we finished the job."

Whit and I are carrying the unconscious, wounded—but decidedly *not* dead—Byron Swain across the difficult terrain, and with every step I think I can hear Pearce trailing us.

"Drop it, Wist. I told you. He's *done*. Let's just focus on getting Byron to the river. We're almost there anyway."

"We are?"

My brother nods, hiking Byron up, and my mind whirs. The only thing in my line of vision is the steep hill we're trudging up, shadows snaking together in the dry grass. Behind us, the dark presence of the bone forest looms. But what's beyond the hill?

I quicken my pace, struggling against Byron's weight to climb higher, faster. I'm light-headed. I didn't believe we'd really get here, that I'd ever see my parents again. I know that Whit has already seen them, but I shut out the thought anyway. If I let myself believe in the possibility and it turns out to be a mirage, like every other time we've seen them, I think it will destroy me.

I bite my lip. *No, Wisty. It's not real. Not yet.*

But I find I'm holding my breath anyway, and when we crest the hill, the valley stretching out beneath us, hope blossoms around my heart. I can see the water snaking below, a thick, gray line dividing here and everything after.

And there, next to the river, like in every dream I've had for months, are my parents. Masses of people surround them, crowds upon crowds walking with no place to go, stymied by a raised drawbridge cutting them off from the river, milling about death's waiting room. But there's no mistaking my parents, standing hand in hand, slightly apart from the rest, with heads raised toward the hilltop. Waiting. For me.

The air is so loaded with magic here I can barely breathe, but I leave Byron with Whit and sprint down to them at full speed, tripping over my feet. My heart is racing so fast it's squeezing my chest.

Not real, not real, not real, I whisper to myself, just in case.

But I crash into my fragile-looking father, nearly knocking us both to the ground, and he *is* real. This is really happening.

"Hey, Firecracker," my dad says, his eyes shining, and I totally lose it.

I grab numbly for my mom's papery hand and try to say something to her — *I love you, I missed you,* anything — but the sobs choke out my words, and I'm hyperventilating.

"Shh, shh, sweetheart," Mom whispers, taking my face in her hands and wiping away the tears with her thumbs.

But she's starting to weep herself as she smoothes my matted hair and looks me over, clasping a hand over her mouth. For the first time in a long while I'm aware of all the bruises on my pale skin, the cuts that haven't yet healed, and the disgusting state of my clothes.

She takes me in her arms, rocking me. "My baby, what happened to you?" Her voice quivers.

"It's okay, Mom. I'm okay," I say, but it's not that convincing since I'm still crying. And still racked with confusion.

I pull away from her. "Why would you tell us not to come for you?" I look at both my parents. They don't answer, but now that I've asked, and now that I'm here, it already doesn't matter. I bury my face in Dad's arms and grip Mom's waist. Now I'm never, ever letting them go again.

"Can I join the happy reunion?" Whit says, looking at all of our puffy eyes and sad faces. I laugh weakly but hold out an arm to my brother. He squeezes my hand and enters the circle, ducking his head to hide his emotion. Tears are streaming freely down my dad's gaunt cheeks.

The four of us stay like that, rocking and hugging, until I feel my mom shiver and I notice the goose bumps erupting on my own arms. A cool wind is picking up, and fast.

"Oh no," a familiar voice moans from nearby. *Celia!* It's always so good to see her, and I want to embrace her, but the look on her face makes me stop.

"Wha—?" I start to ask, but then I understand.

As the temperature plummets, my teeth start to chatter, and I feel a terrible coldness clutching at me—a deeper cold than I've ever felt in the Shadowland before....

It's The One.

Chapter 77

Wisty

THE WIND WHIPS my red hair into my face, and he walks calmly through the valley, his eyes clear and his resolve evident. He seems to glide toward us, the air bending around him, warping as if heat is blowing through it; even the red sky darkens in response to his unwelcome presence. Despite the wind, the river *stops,* the water still as ice.

Everything is *wrong.*

The thousands of spirits fall silent as The One Who Is The One passes, and they step back, eyes lowered in reverence or fear. There is no difference anymore.

He moves through the crowd with deliberate slowness, never taking his gaze from my face.

I lean closer to my family, clutching my mom's delicate arm. My dad stands in front of me, jaw set, and my brother squeezes my shoulder. Celia stands resolutely by his side, her Half-light flickering. We are united, or at least that's how we look. But The One keeps right on coming. And we all know he's coming for *me*.

"So we meet again, Allgoods," The One says cordially, stopping in front of us on the wet gravel. He's alone. "You found the River of Forever. Well, that's fortunate. I couldn't have planned it any better myself."

No one says anything for a moment, and the air feels so heavy I think I'm choking. My parents seem small by my side in the shadow of his towering height. I can't let him hurt them again. Not when it's me he's come for.

"Maybe you didn't plan it. Maybe *we* did," I answer, stepping out from behind my father. My stomach feels like I've been eating rocks.

Whit's fists are balled up defensively. "What do you want?" he spits at The One, and I shake my head. *Whit, don't. This is not just Pearce we're dealing with.*

The One shakes his head as if he's disappointed. "You know what I want. I want the girl with the flaming red hair. I want her fire, I want her energy, I want her *Gift*."

"Never." I shake my head bitterly, my temper already making my body heat up. "You'll have to kill me first." I realize that might be a very real possibility in this situation.

"I don't think you've heard me correctly, child. The time has come. With the four elements under my power—earth, wind, water, and finally, at last, sweet fire—I will be eternal, a *god*."

I can't help but remember what Mrs. Highsmith said to us back in her apartment: our mission is to guarantee that

The One can never play God. Then I think of Pearl's small voice. Maybe she's right; maybe he's already there.

"And once I have that last little requirement"—The One's eyes flash—"my journey will be complete. I've been patient, Wisteria, but I think I've waited for you quite long enough."

I swallow. The time *has* come, but that doesn't mean I have to give in without a fight...right?

"But the Allgoods' journey is also about to be complete!" Dad shouts out of nowhere. I stare at him, surprised. Does he mean *complete*—as in, *ending in our deaths?*

The One is thinking the same thing. "I'm glad we're in agreement about that, Allgood," he scoffs. "This is, indeed, the end. Let's get it over with, shall we? Wisteria?"

He raises an eyebrow, and a dull ache begins near my left temple as the wind whines. He's causing the pain, I'm sure of it. I shiver, unable to answer him. I have absolutely no plan.

Then my mom steps forward, her face hard, defiant. "Our kids"—she puts her arms around Whit's and my waists, hugging us close—"have now passed through the Five Realms. You do realize what this means?"

I sure don't, but everyone else seems to. From their cowed positions crouched along the bank, the hordes of dead souls murmur at the possibility of what she's suggesting, their whispers flitting through the air like moths' wings. Thousands of eyes peek up at The One's face, waiting, waiting.

Naturally, The One just smiles indulgently, amused. "Come now, Eliza, I expected more from you. You don't really believe that little fairy tale, do you?"

The wind howls louder, a testament to his power.

My mom's cheeks redden with the insult. She's inches from him, and though he towers over her tiny, starved body, the look on her face could crush mountains. "The *Prophecies*—which, you'll remember, correctly predicted their Gifts—have been fulfilled," she emphasizes, her voice acidic. "The children have already experienced the Five Realms of human existence: true love, true grief, true fear, true compassion, and, now, true courage. Their rule is at hand."

Wait...*what?* I gape at Whit. His face is a stone mask, but his eyes seem to falter for a moment. Five Realms? Rule? This feels like the first time we're hearing this. Isn't it impossible enough just to dethrone The One and get things back to normal? So we've actually been on some kind of prophetic scavenger hunt ending in a mind-boggling amount of responsibility, and no one bothered to let us in on the real goal?

My head is throbbing now from The One's draw on my power, and his eyes flick to my face as I wince. His serene expression makes me doubt everything all over again. He's so *sure* that he'll win, that we'll all die. How can my parents be so confident in the face of his manipulation?

"Ah yes, the Prophecies," The One considers. "But as you point out, Benjamin and Eliza, they are just children.

283

Unprepared by their parents to do much in the world. Certainly not prepared to rule anyone, or even control the tremendous Gifts they've been given. How does it feel to have failed them?"

Whit and I both step forward and start to protest—much to The One's delight—but my mom waves us off, undeterred.

"If we had revealed Whit's and Wisty's roles to them earlier," she argues, "they could never have truly opened their hearts to the full spectrum of human experience. They would've always felt *other*. They needed to come here, they needed to seek us out against all odds—against death itself—to experience the final level of human experience: courage."

I get it now. This is why our parents told us not to come here: we had to make the choice on our own, despite the risks, to be truly courageous. We resented them so much for not telling us. But they had it right.

"They've achieved something you never will," Dad points out. I get that all of this is a bit over our heads, but I wish they would stop talking about Whit and me like we're not even here. But Dad goes on giving it to The One: "You've sabotaged yourself, killed every bit of compassion you might have had, so you can never experience true love."

"He who controls all the elements is the ultimate ruler." The One snaps his wrist dismissively, and the wind groans. It feels like the air is surging through my skull, and my headache worsens. "We all know how this is going to end, and I'm losing my patience." He steps toward me. "Wisteria, give The Gift to me—*now!*"

As if I even know how to hand over this so-called Gift! Whit and I are just pawns here, and we don't understand the rules of the game. We don't even know what game we're playing.

"Fine!" I yell in a tantrum of exasperation. Fire leaps from my fingertips to The One's crisp suit. It's extinguished immediately, but he looks truly angry for the first time, and I instinctively take a step back.

"Did you forget what Byron taught you, dear girl? You made a grave mistake earlier. You may have paralyzed me for a moment, but your magic only makes me stronger."

I try not to flinch as The One fixes me with his hypnotic eyes. He's smiling like a grandfather about to deliver sage advice. That smile would make a baby weep.

Storm clouds whip around us, but the rain doesn't come. Not yet. The terrified crowd leans forward, and the moment is pregnant with possibility.

The One moves toward me.

"You're *nothing!*" he shrieks directly into my face, sounding unhinged, and sharp, blinding migraine pain flashes behind my eyes.

Like lightning, I think, and I finally begin to understand what this is all about.

Chapter 78

Wisty

THE ONE RAISES his arms, and the elements respond at once to his call....

The earth shakes as a seam splits along the ground, knocking my parents off their feet as they scramble from its widening lip. Dust particles dance in the air as the ground crumbles inward, and the layers of red clouds darken and multiply as the wind rages, making the once-still river begin to churn and foam. The hill running down from the bone forest seems to grow before our eyes, and it belches and groans as lava bubbles over its surface.

It's utter pandemonium as everyone scrambles and lurches to stay out of the way of flooding water and falling rock. My dad pulls me to him, and Whit and Celia lead us higher on the bank. The masses huddle and cry out against the onslaught. Most of the people here are already dead, but apparently death does not kill fear.

The only person who is unafraid, it seems, is my mother.

Mom is weak, tottering, half dead, but she's still a force to be reckoned with as she steps toward The One once again. Her eyes narrow.

"You say you stand for order, for what is right, but you've interrupted the natural order of things, the rhythm and flow of everything that makes us human in life and in death." My mom is a born public speaker, and her voice echoes across the audience of the dead. "Even here at this sacred river, no one can cross over because of what you've done."

Mom's voice rises, full of conviction and courage. "*You* are nothing!" she shouts at The One Who Is The One, ruler of the entire Overworld, and now, it seems, the Underworld, too. Even if we die in the next moment, I have never been more proud of her.

"How dare you." The One's voice is low, deadly. I almost don't hear it above the rising wind. My mom doesn't flinch and stands tall and proud next to the other wavering souls of the dead on this gravelly bank. "You once had such potential yourself, Eliza. And now look at you — barely a bag of bones. Didn't I already kill you once?"

Mom reaches for Dad's arm but never gets that far. She's suddenly, violently ripped from the earth as if by an invisible hand and flung high into the air among the ominous clouds. She twists, her face a grimace, her body shaken and slammed against an invisible wall. As she writhes in agony above our heads, not a soul can turn away from the gruesome theater.

Which is exactly what he wants. To break us.

"He's going to snap her neck!" Dad yells.

I feel panicked, out of control as The One whips our mother back and forth across the sky like a shooting star. I said I'd never lose her again. . . .

Think, Wisty. Use your power, your Gift. My mind races. Fire . . . a shooting star . . .

That's it! I grip my brother's hand and pull everything I can from Whit's M. I feel it shifting, building, growing within me, light and heat and electricity expanding until my power erupts from my fingertips. I stare, breathless.

Together we've created a giant, burning mass of rock surging across the sky.

The crowd gasps as a shower of sparks trails behind the meteor. It's terrifying and blindingly beautiful at once — the most spectacular firework anyone has ever seen.

I've never attempted anything on this scale, and I'm almost scared that it worked. I wince and heave. It's kind of like trying to hold a giant umbrella open in the middle of a hurricane — nearly impossible to control. This thing is barreling toward us at startling speed, and I'm not sure I can steer it where it needs to go. I'm straining so hard that a shriek escapes from my pressed lips.

Whit sends another powerful surge of M through me, and at the last second I manage to jackknife the fireball away from the crowd, sending it careering directly to where The One is standing.

Only he isn't standing there anymore.

Instead it plows straight into the crack in the earth that The One's quake left. The ground shakes, and people are strewn helter-skelter. The impact missed The One entirely, but the distraction breaks his connection with my mother.

Which means her limp, rag-doll body is falling rapidly through the air.

"Mom!" I scream.

But as I watch, her descent slows, and she floats down as if immersed in water. Whit catches her feather body easily in his arms and cradles her close. He nods at me, and tears of relief well in my eyes. His M is strong. I should've known my brother would never let me down when Mom was at stake.

"A mere parlor trick!" exclaims The One. At least I think it's The One. It's his voice, but it's somehow deeper, bigger. And it's coming from all around.

Where is he?

It's like . . . he's everywhere. He's the weather itself, he's every disaster rolled into One. Thunder, wind, earthquake, volcano . . . and now, as the clouds burst, the steady, sting-ing downpour of rain.

I'm dizzy, weakened from the M expended on the meteor, and my head is in such excruciating pain I can barely stand.

Something is changing.

I look to Whit for support, but I can't see him. I can't see anything but light, but I can feel the tug of the elements inside my skull, all of them pulling for one thing, one jolt of static, one frenetic spark....

One bolt of lightning—fire. *My* fire.

By using the elements to create every condition to force lightning to strike, *he can suck The Gift right out of me.*

I feel something in me opening up, seeping out. *It's happening. It's all happening,* I think through the pain and confusion.

And then...

Chapter 79

Whit

IT HAPPENS IN seconds.

The pregnant clouds loom over us, thick and ominous, dark shadows appearing on our faces. It starts to rain.

In the next moment, my sister is no longer my sister.

Her eyes roll back into her head, and foam gathers at the corners of her lips.

Bolts of electricity light up the red sky, and Wisty's body shakes and shudders. The lightning is coming from her—from her Gift—but she's not controlling it.

He is.

"Wisty, *no!*" I shriek, lunging forward. My dad's strong arms hold me back.

"Don't touch her, Whit!" my mom sobs. "I can't lose you, too!" There is nothing any of us can do except watch as my sister's power surges into the sky, taking her with it.

But I can't watch. I have to figure out what to do, how to stop this...thing. I turn away, stumbling over myself, but it's all happening too fast, too certainly, too powerfully. I can't decide what to do because all I *can* do is react.

Pellets of rain pound into us, along with sand and gravel kicked up by the wind.

The frothy waves of the river writhe like a bundle of snakes, the foam rising higher and higher before finally spilling over the shore and flooding the valley, carrying people away or pulling them under, even as I grab for them. The water crashes relentlessly into the bridge, finally splintering its supports and dragging it into the murky depths.

"No!" Celia shouts over the howling wind, stumbling forward, her hand outstretched. It's too late. The plaintive cries of other souls join hers. Without that bridge, no one will ever be able to cross over again.

I turn away from her pain, unable to help her right now. Because if I don't focus on the seam in the earth, which is getting deeper, wider, longer in mere seconds, running along the ground like an animal chasing our feet, I'll be swallowed up.

My mother and father lurch and stumble, following the crowds to higher ground. At least there are no buildings to crush us in this forsaken place.

It's all I can do to lock my knees against the thrashing wind and shut my eyes against the spray of water as the river churns cylindrically upward into the swirling waterspout of a tornado.

And the whole time, my sister is a trembling, electrified zombie at the whim of a madman.

Do something, Whit.

I don't know where to go when everywhere I turn is death. I don't even know what I'm fighting. How can you target the air, the water, the earth, all at once without ever being able to see the person who's doing the damage?

Do *something.*

I guess I target the magic.

I squeeze my eyes tight against the nightmare, concentrate on fixing the damage done, on healing the wounded. On repairing the bridge. On the open gash of the earthquake closing like a slow zipper, the rocks shifting and groaning. On The One turning to smoke, hoping his reign will end the way he vaporized so many innocents before him.

But it doesn't work, not without Wisty, and when I open my eyes, it's getting worse: a frigid, unseen hand is sweeping over everything.

Icy air blasts along the shoreline, and I follow with my eyes as the river freezes over, inch by inch. Hail tears through the sky, pelting down in sharp, relentless sheets that cut into my flesh. My breath billows in front of me, and ice crackles in my wet hair.

The valley is a luminous masterpiece, an ice world glistening under the red clouds. It's breathtaking.

But the implications of The One's power are devastating: *Hell really has frozen over.*

Chapter 80

Whit

THEN, AS IN every situation I think is hopeless, Celia appears at my side.

"Whit, I think I can help," she says, her glow seeming brighter in the chaotic darkness. I feel better with her here even as we brace against the unfathomable wind and debris.

And then I remember the power of the Half-lights. "Can you bring them? Can they defeat the darkness like they did before?" I shout over the raging weather and the screaming of the multitudes.

"No," she answers. "It doesn't work like that, not against an evil so complete."

"What can you do, then?" I nearly wail. I'm freezing, soaked to the bone in the land of the dead, and my sister is still hovering next to the river, power surging out of her as The One holds her in his iron clutches.

This is the definition of *desperate*.

"I can't explain," Celia says. "This is personal, Whit. You don't understand. He...he came into my cell late at night. He came to my bedside."

"What do you mean? Did he—?" I feel sick.

"No, Whit. He's the one who murdered me!" she yells. "He strangled me with his bare hands. He killed me—to get to the two of you."

I'm speechless. And *angry*. My hands shake with the effort of containing my fury. I understand why Celia needs her vengeance.

Before I can ask what she's going to do, she runs. Away from me. Toward him. *It*.

"No, Celia, not like this!" I cry out. She doesn't listen.

She hurls herself into the eye of the storm. *Into The One*.

She disappears right into his evil, swirling mass, and in seconds the storm has absorbed her like another small fleck of sand.

I lurch forward, screaming her name.

But she's gone. Consumed.

Chapter 81

Wisty

I WAKE UP lying on the hard, icy ground, feeling like I've been beaten up but oddly rejuvenated.

The Shadowland is in utter turmoil, with dead people stumbling around screaming and hail tearing through the air.

I spot Whit sobbing farther downstream. I make my way over to him, still kind of dazed, and when I touch his shoulder, he jumps, his eyes nearly popping out of his head. He's staring at me like I'm a monster, and I suppose I look like one.

"Wisty?" he croaks, touching my face, unbelieving. He envelops me in his arms and then holds me back to look at me again. "Wist, excuse me, but...how...how the heck are you still alive?"

"Not really sure about that," I admit. "Are *you* okay?" I eye his dirty, tear-stained face.

"He took Celia," my brother says, and his face is distorted with grief. "I mean…she sacrificed herself. I think she saved your life. It must've broken the connection. It's all over…" Whit trails off, his speech disjointed with shock.

I feel awful about Celia, but what he's just told me makes me realize something: we still have a chance.

"It's not over, Whit. Not by a long shot. If I can survive prolonged electrocution and you can survive losing the person you love the most, it just proves we're getting stronger. We're finally ready, finally strong enough to end him."

"And if it doesn't work?" Whit asks, his voice already defeated. "Are you ready for our own end as well?"

"Yes," I answer. What other choice do I have? This is the Prophecy; this is our purpose. And if we fail…well, life's not going to be worth living anyway. "Are you?" I whisper.

"If it means joining her, yeah," Whit says, and my heart breaks for him.

But there's nowhere to go but forward. "One last shot?" I ask.

"Let's do this, little sis." Whit nods, reliable until the very end, always willing to do anything it takes.

So, once again, Whit and I turn to face this world crumbling around us. We face our nemesis, The One Who Is The One, The One Who Wants To Play God, The One Who Disturbed The Order Of The Whole World, The One Who Must Pay.

If we go down, it'll be in a blaze of glory.

"Ready?" I ask Whit.

"As ever," he replies.

"Go!"

I erupt into flame, and it's my most epic fireball yet. I feel like a small sun rolling toward the river of ice, and the hail turns to light rain as my warmth hits the air. The heat around me is more intense than any I've ever generated, and the crowds of spirits shield their eyes from the blinding blue-and-white flames licking at their faces. My fire rises higher and higher, vaporizing The One's ice into sizzling clouds of effervescent beauty.

It's awesome!

Whit uses his healing power to repair the drawbridge, the broken earth, and the mutilated bodies along the shore.

We're doing so much, so fast, it feels like we're unstoppable for a moment, but I can already feel our power waning as the tornado, still swirling, rakes its way toward us, driving up dirt and sand and growing by the second as it shrieks its tantrum. It towers above us, a ferocious monster pulling us with powerful magnetism into its dark depths.

Whit and I stare upward, mouths slack. We can't even see the top.

I grip my brother's hand, and we face our fate, but Whit's heart isn't in it without Celia, and I'm half afraid he's going to throw himself into that writhing, churning mass of debris and be consumed as well. His face is crumbling, disintegrating, then his eyes shut tight as if he's going to explode in pain.

I see the situation spiraling out of control. Without Whit, we'll lose our edge. That I know.

"Keep fighting, Whit!" I scream at my brother over the howl of the storm. "With everything you have. For Mom's sake, for Dad's sake." He's still not hearing me. "Come on, Whit! Do it for Celia!"

His eyes fly open, his purpose renewed.

And now everyone at the river—my parents; Janine; Emmet and Sasha; all of these spirits and bent, lost souls—chants the immortal words of the Prophecy, eyes shut against the furious wind:

A boy and a girl, fated to rule all. Two will rise, and One will fall.

How can a mere poem, a chant, a Prophecy, compete with this force of evil? It seems insane.

But it's like Whit and I are absorbing all of the strength that has been long buried in these people, and all of the old magic our parents themselves possess. Whit squeezes my hand fiercely, and we throw every ounce of M we have at the beast. The effort of the intense concentration makes my head pound and my arms ache. I feel like sobbing. We're *so* close.

Then, something...magical...happens.

The tornado starts to dissolve, the water and sand and rock and ice falling to the ground as the swirling slows and the eye closes in on itself. I shield my face but focus my M even more intensely. The One's armor falls away, the rain dries up, the raging winds cease their howling.

The One Who Is The One now stands in front of us again, nothing more than a man. He shudders, his eyes dull and unseeing.

"One will fall!" the crowds shout in unison. *"One will fall!"*

The throbbing at my temples becomes almost unbearable, and pain sears again behind my eyes as I focus every ounce of electrical power at him. I feel like I'm in a microwave on high, the colors vibrating all around me in hallucinogenic waves. I'm blacking out.

"ONE! WILL! FALL!"

The One's pupils dilate, his eyes two gaping black holes, and, as if possessed, he croaks, "A single spark!"

And then he just...*dissolves* before our very eyes.

The crimson sky lights up with a bright blast like a bomb exploding, and the pressure lessens and lifts, the power slowly stops flowing from my fingertips, and I feel, for once, free.

It's real.

There's nothing left of Our Great and Noble Leader but a dark, shadowlike stain flickering on the gray-pebbled bank. And, after a moment, even the shadow disappears.

I stare at that patch of ground for a long time. There's really nothing left.

My parents rush to Whit and me, and we're all choking on our tears and squeezing one another tightly, just grateful we're alive. But Whit breaks away from us.

Finally able to have his time to grieve, my brother collapses to his knees on the gravel. "Celia!" Whit yells. "Celia, no! Celia, *please!*" Sobs overtake my poor, wrecked, heartbroken brother, and it feels like the end of everything.

We've defeated The One, like the Prophecy said. The balance has been restored. But it doesn't mean life will go back to the way it was. The One is gone, but many other things are gone, too. Like the parents of so many of these children. Like our homes. Like our innocence. Like our loved ones.

"Come back!" Whit shouts, and I suppress a sob myself. It wasn't supposed to feel like this.

Chapter 82

Whit

SEVERAL SECONDS PASS. No one says a word, and the silence shrieks in my ears like a million wailing ambulances.

But then, as if taking a breath from a short swim, Celia emerges from a wisp of fog, glistening and spectacular. And I start breathing again.

I stand up on shaking legs and try to take her into my arms—her light is so bright it's almost blinding.

I'm still sobbing. With all of that pain, all of that emotion finally unleashed, I wonder if I'll ever be able to stop the torrent of tears again. In front of my parents, and my little sister, and the thousands of people in the crowd who have watched this whole spectacle and think I'm some big hero, I'm choking back hiccuping breaths like a kid.

But I don't care. All I can see is *her.*

"I know, baby," Celia whispers softly, her face so close to mine. "I know."

I can hardly feel her at all, and she's not looking at me like she usually does. It's like she's still far away, less *here.* It's seems like each time I see her, she's less *real.*

The One is gone, so why does everything still feel so very wrong? I don't want to ask her why she's different, why she's looking at me like she's already let us go, because my heart can't take that right now. So instead I ask what every other soul here is wondering: *How could she possibly come back from that writhing mass of One?*

"What did you *do?*" is all I can manage to say.

Celia pulls back from me, slipping through my fingers. "I'm not sure. I think all of our powers were working in reverse. Magic works differently in the Shadowland. We think it passes through here to the Overworld from other realms, so—"

"Talk to me like I'm not going crazy, Celes," I say, groping to find a way to cup her ethereal face. "Even after all that's happened, this is still too much to follow."

"You're able to heal, so you were able to hurt," she goes on. "Wisty can create electrical impulses, so she could shut them down, too. And I..." She pauses, trying to make sense of all of it. "You brought death to his body; Wisty brought it to his mind. And...well, I'm a Half-light, so I'm half life, half death. I think I brought death to his soul."

I'm still trying to process this. "I thought you'd become a *part* of that . . . monster." My voice wavers, the sobs threatening to return.

Celia nods slowly. "In a way, I did." I can't grasp that. "But I needed this, Whit. I needed to pay him back. For stealing my life. For stealing our life together."

Chapter 83

Wisty

THANKS TO MY brother's awesome healing spells, the drawbridge across the River of Forever is back in working order, fully lowered and functional, looking like it never even encountered the wrath of the elements. And with The One's influence gone, the crowds slowly begin to file across again.

The Resistance—Emmet, Janine, Sasha, and the others—are standing downstream, holding hands and grinning at us. Sasha lets out a wild whoop and Emmet's supporting a beaten but not broken Byron, who gives me a wan thumbs-up. I return the signal, and for a while we all watch as the natural order is restored, souls moving on and journeys coming to a close.

I stand with my family, and Feffer runs up and licks my hand. After all this poor pup's been through, she's ready to go home. We all are.

Someone starts softly singing one of the great Forbidden

Hymns, and before long hundreds of people are singing together. The song builds and falls, and the voices are so beautiful you could almost forget we're in the land of the dead. Hearing my mother sing again is almost too amazing for words.

Then Dad motions for Whit to come toward him, and when he does, Dad squeezes him in a ferocious hug.

"You take care of your sister, now, champ," Dad says solemnly. "Like always." He looks at me with a sparkle in his eyes. "And you. I know you'll stay out of trouble, won't you, Wisty? Make your old man proud. Like always."

Every alarm in my head goes off, and my autoimmune responses go nuts. We finally have our parents back. So why is this starting to feel like good-bye?

"Dad?" I squeak, eyes searching and welling with tears, and when he won't meet my gaze: *"Mom?"* I look to her, demanding an answer.

She strokes my hair. "It's our time, sweets. We've been here waiting, just like everybody else. It's time to finally see what's on the other side of that river."

They step forward to join the line of spirits. "To cross over," my dad confirms.

Chapter 84

Wisty

PANIC CONSTRICTS MY chest while adrenaline surges into my ears. I'm pulling at my tangled hair as angry, ugly tears stream freely down my face.

My parents are moving toward the bridge, holding hands, brave, ready to face their fates, just like they were that day at the execution. And just like that day, I feel utterly helpless. Just like that day, I'm going to let my parents slip right through my fingers.

And The One wins. Again.

"Wait!" I shout, the plaintive, sharp edge of the word piercing the air.

Mom and Dad turn, expectant. They are two tiny, anonymous silhouettes against the red gash of sky.

"Just...wait a minute," I whimper softly, my mind racing. "This feels wrong. This is not how it's supposed to go."

"I know, I know, sweetie," my mom coos to me, stroking my hair, trying to calm me down. Placating me.

I brush her hand away. "No! I mean, it *really* feels wrong. It's time, yes, but what if it's time for us to go home again? All of us. *Together.*"

I step between my parents and the crowds of people streaming along the River of Forever. The wind whips against me. *Please,* I chant to myself. *Please. Please.*

"But, honey," Mom reasons, "we're dead. You have to understand that this is what happens next."

"They got it wrong. I just know that it's all wrong," I plead, my eyes burning from the tears. I squeeze my mother's arms. "I can *feel* you. You're not spirits, and you're not Lost Ones. You have substance. How do you explain that?"

My dad looks around at the spirits, at the flowing river flickering through their bodies. "It's true, Eliza. We never lost that, not like...everybody else."

"But how are we still...part of the living?" Mom asks. "I *felt* death. I felt my breath leave my body."

I shake my head, uncertain. "Maybe it has to do with The One. He used that power to...vaporize you...so maybe now that he's gone, the spell is lifted. Maybe now you can go home."

Dad puts his hand in Mom's. "Maybe she's right. Maybe we really can go home. We can certainly try."

"It'll work." I nod vigorously, suddenly relieved, suddenly

more sure of this than I've been of anything in my life: my parents weren't meant to die. At least not that day.

I'm beaming at them, so excited, but something else is wrong.

Whit is looking at Celia with the most heartbreaking expression I've ever seen. Anybody can see that he's hoping the same is true for her. He touches her arm, but it's still flickering somewhere between *here* and *there*.

Not solid.

She shakes her head before he can say anything, and he interlaces his hand with hers. "It could work, Celes. You don't know for sure if—"

"I *know*," she whispers, a single tear sneaking out of her eye. If it were just her and Whit she might break down, but with my whole family watching her guiltily, she sucks it up and takes a deep breath.

"It's not like with your parents, Whit. It wasn't a mistake with me; it wasn't a spell. I was murdered by the hands of a greedy, violent person, and I don't get to come back. I don't get a future. I know you don't want me to go, but—"

"Then why were you a Half-light? You weren't like all of the other spirits at the river, just waiting to cross over. Why would you cross now?" Whit refuses to back down.

"I think I've been stuck in the Shadowland so that I could help you, protect you like you always tried to protect me when I was alive. Having that chance to help destroy

The One *was* my purpose. I know it sounds impossible, but... I'm ready. I'm ready to cross over, to be *all* light."

Whit shakes his head defiantly, and Celia takes his face in both of her hands.

"Yes, baby. It's my time."

Chapter 85

Whit

"YOU'LL SEE ME again someday, Whit. One day you'll have to cross the river yourself."

I cannot do this. I cannot let Celia go. Not again.

"You don't know that. You don't even know what's on the other side, or if we'll ever see each other again. Do you really want to take that chance, Celia? Just leave all this — everything we have — and go into some unknown?"

We walk away from the group, where Sasha is arranging a buddy system for the journey back to the Overworld. Wisty is giving me a look of utter pity, and in the moment I totally resent her for it.

"Whit, don't be like this," Celia says while we're walking. "You know I was never meant to stay here. I think everybody can agree that pale was never a good look for me." She laughs, but it feels forced.

I don't even crack a smile in response, and I'm staring into her eyes solemnly. Celia looks sad but frustrated, too.

She knows that, for the first time ever, I don't want her to have what she wants. I need to be completely selfish for once in my life.

"Come on, baby, do you really want to see me stuck here in this limbo, never able to experience The After, and instead getting weaker and more consumed by death every day?" I won't meet her eyes. "Is that what you really want for me?" she presses.

Yes! I want to shout. *I want you within arm's reach, always. A portal away, stuck in this hell, if it means I don't have to lose you.*

Instead I sigh and shake my head no, feeling guilt and unbearable desire at the same time.

"At least we get to say good-bye this time. Come here."

Celia pulls me close, and for a brief, exhilarating moment, we merge. I feel her light surge through me, more warm, more healing than I could've imagined. My head swirls with love and beauty, and when we part, I think I finally understand.

What we had was so perfect in the world before the New Order, but that isn't the world anymore, and we're not the same people. I can't keep her trapped in this prison just so she can be the idealized version of what I hoped to have.

I'm ready to let her go.

I inhale her sweet scent and bury my face in her curls, and then watch as she walks away from me. No good-byes. That merge was everything we needed to say.

Janine comes up and stands by my side, her hand on the small of my back, comforting me, supporting me as Celia disappears over the bridge, light forming a bright halo around her.

After she crosses, I look down at Janine's face, drained and unbelievably pale. It looks like it's all she can do to keep standing, let alone sustain me.

"Janine!" I shout, alarmed.

It's okay, she mouths, and then collapses into my arms.

EPILOGUE

ALL THAT REMAINS

Chapter 86

Whit

WE PULL UP to the old house, Dad and Mom in the front, me and Wisty bickering over who gets to sit closest to the one functioning window in the back, just like old times. You'd think that after conquering the world's most evil being and restoring peace and order for all, we'd be a little more mature, but sometimes the most comforting thing in the world is being able to hold your kid sister in a headlock and beg your mom to change the radio station already.

We sit in the van for a few minutes—it's the old van from the Resistance days—taking in the neighborhood. The tree I crashed into on my bike, the bush next door where Wisty hid when she ran away, the porch swing where I used to kiss Celia. Mrs. Tillinghast across the street reviving her garden, Mr. Hsu taking the boards off his doors and windows. We're not quite ready to believe we're really here, that all of this is real, that our old lives are where we left them.

I'm aghast. "I thought it was all gone. Wiped out by the New Order."

"Amazing what kind of magic can happen when good triumphs over evil," Dad says seriously. "Never underestimate the difference it can make."

"Stuff actually looks pretty much the same," Wisty quips.

"Yep, even the same leaky pipes, same garage door that sticks, same bathroom needing a coat of paint," Mom says wryly, looking at Dad.

"Yeah, yeah, I'm on it," he replies, but they're both smiling from ear to ear.

He takes her hand, and they turn around in their seats to look at us.

"Do you know how very, very proud of you guys we are?" Mom says, tears glistening in her eyes. "You're the most courageous, compassionate kids—nearly adults—that any parent could ask for."

It sounds cheesy, but Wisty and I are seriously beaming like a couple of morons.

"We owe you so much," Dad continues. "Not just our freedom, or our home, but our *lives,* and each other. Without you we'd be—" My parents lock eyes, and Dad's start to well up.

"Dad, you don't owe us anything." My voice cracks.

My dad shakes his head as if waving the emotion away. "All I'm saying is you did good, kids." He squeezes my shoulder and then Wisty's hand. Tears are streaming down my sister's face.

We sit like that for a minute, just thankful for one another, and then Mom starts laughing and wipes the water off her cheeks.

"So what are we waiting for?" she asks so brightly that we all laugh, too. "Let's get our house back."

Feffer barks her assent from the back, and we follow her out of the van and walk together up to the front steps. Wisty looks up at me, and I nod.

"This is as far as we go," I tell my parents, stopping on the porch.

Mom looks concerned. "You're not leaving already?"

"We have to, Mom," Wisty says, hugging her. "There are still things we have to do out there. Evil didn't die just because The One did."

Dad frowns. "Evil is going to be there anytime you look for it. The work will never be done. Maybe you should take some time to be yourselves, to just be kids for a bit." Wisty looks at me. We both hesitate, but we know what needs to be done.

"It feels like we stopped being kids a long time ago, Pops," I say gently. "You guys let us be kids for as long as you could, and we had an amazing childhood. But now we know who we are—what we are—and that we have a bigger responsibility."

Dad looks at Mom, who nods, pressing her lips together.

I can see the anxiety on their faces, but they know we're making the right call, and they're proud, too. "All right, then. Come back and visit. We'll be here this time. I know you'll take care of each other and trust your instincts, and I hope you'll always follow your hearts."

He turns to me. "And, guys?" My father gives each of us a long look filled with conflict, and I stare at him questioningly. But in the end he just shakes his head decisively and shrugs. "Come here" is all he says, enveloping Wisty and me in a fierce hug. He grips the back of my neck. "Just be careful," he whispers.

"Always." I nod.

As we walk away from our parents once again, I know that there's so much more about this world to understand and learn. But this time, I'm ready.

Chapter 87

Wisty

WHIT AND I pull out of our driveway in our rusty old van that we recovered from the local N.O. OFFICIALS ONLY lot. We may be unsure of where we're going, but we're positive we'll find friends when we get there.

Our street buzzes with activity. There is still evidence of the mass destruction caused by The One—leveled buildings and unused watchtowers casting shadows on the rubble below—but in just a few days since the collapse of the New Order, you can already *feel* change afoot.

For one, there are *people* everywhere. Not soldiers in black boots waving automatic rifles but everyday citizens emerging from behind their blackened windows and repairing their collapsed porches. No longer looking at their neighbors from behind a veil of suspicion. Letting down their cloaks of fear inch by inch.

And as we wave good-bye to Mom and Dad, knowing they'll still be here when we get back, knowing they're not in danger, and knowing how proud they are of their two determined children who just happen to be a witch and a wizard, it feels incredible to roll down the windows, rock out hard to the music blasting on the Free Youth Radio, and breathe in the just-a-little-bit-cleaner air, saturated with a new sense of hope.

Whit turns down the radio and looks at me, all seriousness. "So what's next, Wist? The Prophecies said that we're supposed to lead a new generation, that kids will rule the world…"

I nod, feeling not for the first time the crushing responsibility that has been placed on our shoulders. We dealt with The One, and now we're supposed to just lead the whole world?

Whit continues, "What do you think that means for us *now?* There are all these former New Order zombies walking around dazed, like they don't know what their purpose in life is without The One. If we're not careful, all these drifters are going to turn to anarchic violence."

Though the scenario is completely feasible, I'm still on an optimistic high. For once, Wisty the cynic is preaching about how great things are.

"You're looking at this all wrong, though, Whit. All these people being confused and directionless *isn't* a bad thing. It leaves the door wide open for the Resistance to get organized, focused, and strong."

"You mean take advantage of the situation like The One did."

I give Whit an eye roll that only a little sister can perfect.

"Except we're not The One and we don't have an evil agenda. This is a chance to step up and rehabilitate the land, and to make the *people* count."

Whit nods and stares out at the people on the streets coming together, working to help their neighbors. I smile at a group of children playing in an alley. No N.O. uniforms. No guns. Almost no remnants of the Blood Plague.

"Okay but, Wisty, we really do need more of a plan here if we're going to get anything done. What does 'rehabilitating the land and making the people count' mean for us *today?* What's the first step? How do we make this happen?"

My brother, always the practical one.

I shrug. "Maybe it's through music," I suggest, cranking the radio back up. Whit sighs as I bang my head to the beat, but he's grinning, too.

"I think Wisty makes a good point," Byron pipes up out of nowhere from the backseat. I nearly jump out of my skin, and Whit swerves the van.

"Byron! What the—?" I smack his arm, but Swain just keeps right on inserting his unsolicited opinion as if he's been part of the conversation all along.

"Historically, music has been really successful in uniting groups of people for a common cause. And remember how many kids came out in support of the Resistance at the Stockwood Music Festival? It was...incredible."

His voice takes on a dreamy tone, and I know he's thinking about the electric moment when my power flowed through him and we rocked a stadium packed full of screaming fans. Best night of my life. I'm getting chills thinking of it, too.

But as usual my annoyance with Byron Swain seems to override any other feeling. If he's in the van now, it means he was in here before with Mom and Dad, too.

"You were here the whole time?" I demand. "You spied on our family's most intimate moment?"

Byron nods, and without even hesitating, I zap him right back into weasel form.

"Aw, come on, Wist," the critter squeaks at me, perched on the back of my seat. "You know I only did it because I wanted to get closer to you, learn more about your crazy witchy ways."

"Yeah, keep talking, Byron. Hope you're looking forward to a diet of birds' eggs and mice, because you're going to be a weasel for a *very* long time."

The weasel makes some pathetic squeaking noises, and I start to feel bad for him. His little twitching nose tugs at my heartstrings. I change him back on a whim.

"Thanks," he whispers in my ear, "but I was serious about just wanting to get close to you, Wisty."

Then, before I know what's happening, awkward, annoying, insufferable Byron Weasel Swain leans in for the most tender, electric kiss I could never have even imagined—especially coming from him.

Whit gives a low whistle.

My head spins, my stomach flips, and my heart surges. This can't be good.

"Now, that," I say, dazed, when he finally pulls back, "does not bode well for your future."

Chapter 88

Whit

THE ONE MAY be gone and the New Order may be mostly wiped out, but there is still so much to do.

I turn off the ignition, and Wisty, Byron, Emmet, and Sasha leap out of the van, stretching their legs.

Byron's got his arm around Wisty's waist, and Sasha's giving them both a hard time about it. Wisty's blushing a deep crimson, but I notice she doesn't shrug away from Byron's touch. She looks... like she's having fun. She looks happier than I've seen her since the New Order came and turned everything upside down.

Janine turns to me from the front passenger seat. "By the way, I don't think I've even had a chance to say thank you, for saving my life and healing me back in the Shadowland."

I grin. "We were just going to ditch you back by the river, but I guess I just kinda like having you around."

She laughs, then looks out the window at the scene

awaiting us. "You ready?" she asks, squeezing my hand. I take a deep breath and squeeze back.

"More ready than I've ever been," I say, and we follow the others outside.

The building is not as I remember it. The front door has been replaced, the holes have been patched up, and people are high on ladders, working to rebuild the blown-out upper floors.

Holiday lights sparkle across the balcony, and shiny ornaments wink from windows. The snow globe sits in a place of honor on the porch.

The Needermans peer out from their doorway. Not one looks to the sky for bombs. Their clothes aren't new, but they're newer. Their hope isn't totally restored, but it's being patched up. And they'll do fine. They'll persevere, and thrive. Because that is what survivors do every day of their lives.

Pearl Marie wriggles out from behind Mama May and runs over to us, a goofy smile on her face. She leaps into my arms and throws her hands around my neck.

"You did what you said you would," she marvels. "You actually got us free, just like you promised. That's unbelievable."

"You expected any less, kid? I'm a scary witch," says Wisty, wiggling her fingers. She playfully jabs me in the ribs. "And Whit is a wise old wizard."

I can't help grinning at my kid sister. "See, Pearl Marie? Didn't we tell you we'd come back? Didn't I promise?"

Pearl nods and fixes me with her wide gray eyes, the eyes of a seven-year-old far too jaded for her years but moving tentatively toward trust in the good of the world.

I've never been more relieved to be able to keep a promise.

As we walk through the streets, busy with new life, I get it now. There are no endings, and there are no fairy tales. But the pages keep being written. Time soldiers on.

Who knows if our darkest days are behind us? Or if The One will be the only person to bring them? All I know is, it was all real, every moment.

I can close the book on this part of our history. I can start a new chapter, but it doesn't matter.

Because now, the magic is everywhere.

Excerpts of
NEW ORDER PROPAGANDA

as Disseminated by
The Council of N.O. "Arts"

TRADITIONS AND THE FIGUREHEADS THEREOF WHO PLACE A DEITY ABOVE THE ONE WHO IS THE ONE

as Outlawed by The One Who Manages Traditions, Customs, Rituals, Practices, And Beliefs

<u>Accem</u> (noun, proper):
Millions of people in a pious group made a point to visit this ancient city at least once in their lifetime and to pray, neck-to-floor, five times daily toward its geographic location. The New Order has subsequently banned all compasses so that the position of the previously holy city cannot be traced.

<u>free will</u> (noun):
A delusional idea that humans are in control of their own destiny and not subject to the benevolent rule of The One Who Is The One. Because of the popularity of this disgraceful way of thinking among unenlightened previous generations, citizens today need constant reminders that submission to the New Order is the One true way.

<u>miracles</u> (noun):
Coincidental events that promote excitement and/or belief in false powers or deities higher than The One Who Is The One. All such unexplained events must be deleted from memory straightaway.

<u>Mopus Day</u> (noun, proper):
An ancient tradition that called for the most strict and sterile lifestyle, down to its followers' modest garments and rigid schedule. The New Order found its obstinate worship of a deity other than The One Who Is The One objectionable, and the movement was disbanded, but many of its ascetic traditions have been implemented into everyday life at the Brave New World Center.

<u>pray</u> (verb):
The curious act of acknowledging—and attempting to talk to—a being reported to rank higher than The One Who Is The One. Anyone caught with hands folded together or bowed at the waist on the floor, without reference to The One, will be subject to the most gruesome punishment possible.

Prophecies (noun):
Chantable verses that claim to tell the future, often in unlistenable and unlawful poetry form. *Prophecies* are fabricated nonsense created by rebellious teenagers looking to cause mayhem. It is against the law for such utterances to be passed on in any form, regardless of how ominous they may sound or how clever their rhyme scheme.

The Reformed Nation (noun, proper):
When known Resistance sympathizer Barton Ruthmer posted an excessive list of complaints against the regime on the front door to the New Order palace compound, he was promptly executed. His remaining followers, should there be any left, will be, too.

(MORE) ESPECIALLY OFFENSIVE BOOKS THAT HAVE BEEN BANNED
as Dictated by The One Who Bans Books

THE ADVENTURES OF YINGYING: A silly, young self-employed detective with absurd hair travels the world with his small dog and forces his way into situations where his presence is unwanted. This book's accounts of a common citizen's brazen attempts to take the law into his own hands were loathsome, and the series frequently disregarded the infallible scrutiny involved in passing passport checkpoints. It has been banned from bookshelves to avoid any more fantastical errors.

BACKWARD STORIES FROM RESISTANCE SCHOOL: Twenty chapters profile twenty outlandish classmates in a traitorous school that lectures students about fighting the New Order regime, and recounts the bloopers of failed missions along the way. Using this treacherous book as evidence, N.O. soldiers located the school and destroyed it.

THE MYSTERIOUS DERELICT CIVILIZATION: A group of four children run about the ruins of an ancient office building once belonging to a corporation called Apfel, searching for clues about the rise and fall of its domineering yet completely shrouded empire. After the book's publication, the author was gently reminded that there are perfectly good reasons why history has been erased, and such curiosity should be nipped in the bud.

STEVE PLYMOUTH: An adventure about an overly emotional, ineffectual young New Order recruit who must kill the ex-boyfriends of the young New Orderling of his dreams before they can be together. Although a solid take on the need for toughening up young recruits, the plot relied too much on romance and popular culture; the book is therefore banned.

THE SHADOWICK CHRONICLES: Twin boys move into their great-aunt's Victorian home in what the previously uninformed author claims to be the Shadowland (a mythical location that the New Order has gone to great lengths to prove does not exist). NOTE: The author of *The Shadowick Chronicles* has since been convincingly reinformed of the imaginary nature of "the Shadowland."

A CRINKLE IN THE MIND: Three siblings develop so-called magical powers that allow them to bend time. They use this power to escape the current government and explore new and far inferior worlds. If these children were not fictional, they would already be on their way to one of the New Order's many reformatories for confused and dangerous citizens.

THE SUSIE DARKSHACK SERIES: A woman in her twenties lives in a small town where her peers are humans and demons (made-up beings very likely created by would-be witches and wizards to terrify the respectable citizens of the New Order). She struggles to find a balance between which "demons" she should leave alive and well for her social life, and which she should kill off to maintain her safety. The obvious answer is that all manifestations of fictional beings should be destroyed without delay.

PROHIBITED WEBSITES MEANT FOR SUBTERFUGE
as Proclaimed by The One Who Surfs The Cyberspace

Critter: A virtually incomprehensible online system of short, cryptic messages that helped Resistance fighters exchange hazardous information with one another. New Order efforts to eliminate this exceedingly criminal means of communication were swift and absolute.

Juggle: This search engine was invented by a young rebel who narcissistically believed she could create a record of every piece of illegal, duplicitous, and highly dangerous information on the Internet. WARN-ING: This young woman is still at large and attempting to supply the good citizens of the New Order with so-called free-speech documents that contain false propaganda against The One and your illustrious government. A reward is offered for her capture.

MyTaste: A social hub where users glorified the vice of individuality, based on their literary and musical tastes, to one another for "fun." The New Order swiftly realized how much banned material was being distributed on the site and took action to replace all unlawful forms of "creative content" with acceptable New Order documents, such as the *New Order Citizens' Code* and the autobiography of our esteemed leader, *How I Became The One*.

Countenance Digest: This site contained the complete history of an age where children and adults were free to disseminate information—cultural notes, events, political opinions, photos, and other poisonous freedoms—through a massive user-generated publication. All traces of its existence have been ordered deleted from every computer's cache.

INAPPROPRIATE TELECASTS THAT PROMOTE ABSURDITY AND DELUSIONS OF GRANDEUR
as Shut Down by The One Who Restructures The Visual Media

FLEE: A musical comedy about Resistance kids attempting to escape from the Brave New World Center. The children realize that by singing inane pop songs in captivity, they are able to inflict massive psychological torture on their captors. Highly inappropriate material.

DISAPPEARED: This drama follows a group of Resistance rebels whose plane—successfully tampered with by brave New Order soldiers—crashes into a deserted island. The passengers are subjected to tests by what they believe is a "magical" island (really a controlled space created by specialist New Order scientists), only to find that they are being held there until they can be executed for their crimes against the government. A fitting end for criminals of the state, but as the show inspired many rogue counter-telecasts with an anti–New Order message, it was discontinued.

THE HOSPICE: A hospital mockumentary chronicling the daily lives of the last people alive who can still remember the time before being ruled by The One Who Is The One. The hospital's insufferable manager, Melvin Slott, tries to make their last days easier, but for some reason each patient's health deteriorates drastically under his care.

SAWS AND MOLDER: A documentary that goes behind the scenes of New Order prisons through hidden cameras in interrogation chambers, with events displayed each week to the public. While intended by the Resistance movement as a so-called exposé, these tapes have been embraced by The One as a means to bring the good people of the New Order together against the criminals that threaten us. All cameras have since been disabled, but reruns of the original recordings can be found on New Order network channels.

THE REAL CHURLS: The true story of seven captured Resistance teenagers picked to live in a beautiful government palace and have their lives taped to see if specialized New Order training could put them on the right path. As the show became increasingly violent due to the nature of the aggressive, uneducated participants, the experiment had to be abandoned.

WHO WANTS TO BE THE ONE WHO IS THE ONE?: A popular game show that fed contestants trivia questions and promised its winners a chance at the throne for a day. No one managed to earn the top prize before the show was removed from the airwaves, due to objections from The One Who Is The One.

ANGEL
A MAXIMUM RIDE NOVEL

James Patterson

HOW DO YOU SAVE EVERYTHING AND EVERYONE YOU LOVE . . .

Max Ride and her best friends have always had one another's backs. No matter what. Living on the edge as fugitives, they never had a choice. But now they're up against a mysterious and deadly force that's racing across the globe – and just when they need one another the most, Fang is gone. He's creating his own gang that will replace everyone – including Max.

WHEN YOU CAN'T BE TOGETHER . . .

Max is heartbroken over losing Fang, her soulmate, her closest friend. But with Dylan ready and willing to fight by her side, she can no longer deny that his incredible intensity draws her in.

BUT YOU CAN'T STAY APART?

Max, Dylan, and the rest of their friends must soon join with Fang and his new gang for an explosive showdown in Paris. It's unlike anything you've ever imagined . . . or read.

AN ILLUSTRATED NOVEL

Middle School
The Worst Years of My Life

James Patterson
& Chris Tebbetts

Illustrated by Laura Park

Rafe Khatchadorian has enough problems at home without throwing his first year of middle school into the mix. Luckily, he's got an ace plan for the best year ever, if only he can pull it off. With his best friend Leonardo the Silent awarding him points, Rafe tries to break every rule in his school's Code of Conduct. Chewing gum in class – 5,000 points! Running in the hallway – 10,000 points! Pulling the fire alarm – 50,000 points! But when Rafe's game starts to catch up with him, he'll have to decide if winning is all that matters, or if he's finally ready to face the rules, bullies, and truths he's been avoiding.

Containing over 100 brilliant illustrations, *Middle School* is the hilarious story of Rafe's attempt to somehow survive the very worst year of his life!

We support

National
Literacy
Trust

I'm proud to be working with the National Literacy Trust, a great charity that wants to inspire a love of reading.

If you loved this book, don't keep it to yourself. Recommend it to a friend or family member who might enjoy it too. Sharing reading together can be more rewarding than just doing it alone, and is a great way to help other people to read.

Reading is a great way to let your imagination run riot – picking up a book gives you the chance to escape to a whole new world and make of it what you wish. If you're not sure what else to read, start with the things you love. Whether that's bikes, spies, animals, bugs, football, aliens or anything else besides. There'll always be something out there for you.

Could you inspire others to get reading? If so, then you might make a great Reading Champion. Reading Champions is a reading scheme run by the National Literacy Trust. Ask your school to sign up today by visiting www.readingchampions.org.uk.

Happy Reading!

James Patterson